# Possum Crossing

## *A Tale of a Place in West Virginia*

**Leigh Anne Cooper**

authorHOUSE®

*AuthorHouse™*
*1663 Liberty Drive*
*Bloomington, IN 47403*
*www.authorhouse.com*
*Phone: 1 (800) 839-8640*

*Published by AuthorHouse  02/03/2017*

*ISBN: 978-1-5246-7036-8 (sc)*
*ISBN: 978-1-5246-7037-5 (hc)*
*ISBN: 978-1-5246-7035-1 (e)*

## *Acknowledgement*

*To H.B.:*

Without your encouragement and assistance *Possum Crossing* would still be a mere dream.

# Contents

# Preface

Have you ever heard of people who claim to have died, seen heaven and have come back to tell about it? Well, this story is about a real heaven and it's located right here on earth. There're no angels or folks floating around in space. There're no streets paved with gold or harps playing twenty-four hours per day.

You'll find real life people living out their days just like you do. These are good people making their way in a good place. As they say on the TV and in the movies the stories you are about to read are all true accounts but the names have been changed to protect individuals' privacy and, of course, to avoid the potential wrath of lawyers wanting to make a quick buck. I cannot attest to the fact that all the events happened in my lifetime here in Possum Crossing. Being that as it may, I can say I have heard these stories just as you would expect in small town America, many of which I've witnessed with my own eyes. Therefore, you may reasonably accept them as true.

You may be familiar with some of the stories since they are not necessarily restricted to our town but you may not be aware that all these things are happening around you. There is a cancer eating away at the heart of America and hopefully your awareness of it will hasten the demise of this disease. Good people should be treated as such by those who govern them. Leaders may have had the best of intentions when they introduced this deadly killer but they must realize the folly of what they have done and set about correcting it.

Keep in mind that these are good people who were once a proud people. However, they have been betrayed by those who sent them down this path.

The narrator will acquaint you with them and through them with their town, Possum Crossing, West Virginia, United States of America.

## Chapter I Go West Young Man

Possum Crossing, West (by God) Virginia is jest about the best little town in America. No, in the whole world; make that the entire ever expandin multiple big bang universe. I wuz born here, grew up here, raised my family here and intend to die here, Good Lord willin.

Lots of you livin on the coasts of America probably know West Virginia only for coal mines and decayin rust belt areas. You don't know West Virginia as the Switzerland of America. There's beauty in them there mountains and plenty of fishin, hikin, kayakin and even skiin in the winter. Take a tour sometime and you'll find one of the most beautifulest places on earth. Why do you spend thousands to go on cruises and trips to far away places when you haven't even seen the natural beauty God has placed right here in the heart of the USA? Look at a map of the USA. Where do you find West Virginia? Right where the very heart should be. Why the state is almost shaped like a heart. Our panhandles are like major arteries that extend north and east pumpin commerce, which is the life blood of America. Durin the Civil War the country needed us to protect the route of the Baltimore and Ohio Railroad, a major asset crucial to America's economy. You big city folks have skyscrapers, theaters, symphony orchestras, professional sport teams and the like but there is jest somethin missin. I traveled to Morgantown onest and I wuz never so glad to git back home to Possum. Possum is what us locals call Possum Crossing when we is talkin about our town. It seems to be comfortin to think of it that way. It's our Possum.

Possum Crossing got its name when Noah McCorkle decided to leave the family farm in the Shenandoah Valley of Virginia and strike out for the west. The McCorkles had farmed in the valley for as long as anyone could remember. Adam, head of the family and a stern taskmaster, kept his five boys busy with farm chores. It provided a livin for the boys and their families who lived on the property. Bein a #3 son, Noah wuz a bit of a rebel in the clan. He longed to strike out for hisself and make his way on the frontier in the West. West wuz the rich farm lands of the Ohio territory where you could stake your claim to acres of land to start a new life. You were your own boss and success or failure wuz on your own shoulders.

Noah had reached the limit of arguin with his Pa about his compensation for workin on the farm and his desire to own his land for hisself. He and wife Nancy Sue had three children now (all boys) and another wuz on the way or "in the oven" as they wuz want to say. They needed more to supply their needs and his Pa wuz one who squoze a penny till it darn near melted in his hand. He wuzn't about to take no sass from a spunkin dissatisfied child. Stay under the thumb or git off the farm and do what you please. Adam wuz the boss and he intended that it remain so.

So Noah and Nancy Sue packed what little household goods they had into the wagon; they hitched the mules and tossed the boys with the dog into the space that remained. Westward they headed full of joy and hopefulness about what lay ahead. Ohio, the land you dreamed about, wuz jest over the mountains and across the beautiful Ohio River. Farmin would be good there and best of all you kept the fruits of your labor. They bounced their way over the dusty and sometimes muddy trail till they were within sight of that mighty River. There wuz times when it meandered along the border between Virginia and the Ohio territory but this time it wuz aragin when they approached the shoreline. Spring rains had not only made the trail muddy, full of ruts, and darn near impassible but the Ohio wuz showin the might of fast movin waters wider than the river bed could contain. The spring rains kept acomin and the creeks which fed the river were also filled with waters rushin to join up with the Ohio on its way to marryin up with the mighty Mississippi.

They wuz days lookin for a place to cross and jest about wonderin if this adventure had been a mistake when young McCorkle spotted what he figured wuz a good luck omen. Their wagon wuz strainin to keep goin when an opossum crossed the trail jest a few feet in front of the mules.

"This is it! This is a sign from the Almighty that this here is where we start our new life. Hell, Ohio don't look no better from where I sit here on this wagon," McCorkle, weary from the trip and soaked from the rain, declared.

Noah McCorkle wuz right. Either side of the river wuz jest about the same in appearance. Lush green landscape and access to plenty of good, clean water. The Lord had sent the possum to mark the spot and now they could set about makin their new home. No need to risk crossin the rushin water, no need to even leave Virginia. Jest up the rollin hill wuz all the farmland you could ever want in your deepest wishes of the heart. It wuz so close to the Ohio territory you could almost sense the heartbeat of the frontier.

Nancy Sue wuz relieved that the trip would be over. Now they would set about buildin their cabin. There wuz plenty of timber and she could imagine her home standin in sight of the river and Ohio territory. Things would be ready by the time the little one arrived and the humble cabin could be turned into a fine home for her baby, the boys and Noah. And it worked out jest as she had imagined and the good Lord had planned, for the farm prospered and they found mighty fine times. Course the family continued to grow. Abraham, Benjamin, Caleb were soon joined by Daisey Sue. Then along came Ethan, George and finally the sweetest of them all, little Hannah. Noah had named them all: A, B, C, D, E, G, and H. Better to keep track to them all that way. Oh, no 'F.' Noah hated failure more than a man could imagine. 'F' meant failure. There'd be no 'F' in his family. Nancy wuz so proud her youngins were alive and kickin that she let Noah do all the namin. She wuz obedient to her man jest like it said in the Good Book. Sides, he had to do the callin for the chores so they had best have names he could remember.

As the years passed, the farm grew and grew. Corn stood taller than a man and the rows stretched to the tops of hills. There wuz horses, cows, pigs, goats and chickens runnin about everywhere on the property. Crops grew easily and the barn wuz always full to the rafters. When tales of prosperity spread, lots of other settlers came by too. Possum stood as Noah had named the location where the family found paradise. Possum farm wuz paradise also to the growin number of settlers headin for the Ohio territory. So much so that Ohio soon became a state. Jest like ole Virginnie, a star in the flag. It was a new century and the 1800's promised to be good for Noah and the family.

Shortly after Ben growed to be a man he set to helpin folks wishin to cross the river. That's when he and Abe set up the Possum Fairyboat River Crossin Co. The fairy wuz a way for the boys to strike out and make it on their own. It went way beyond what the boys had hoped for. Everyone headin west needed to git to Ohio and the service wuz pleased to accommodate. Horses, mules, cattle, wagons and people were transported across the river to Ohio. Twernt long afore there wuz a blacksmith and livery stable and an inn of sorts for folks to rest a bit after a trek across the Alleghenies. Folks jest kept acomin and the town jest kept agrowin since many decided to put down roots on the eastern side of the river. Why, there wuz soon a bank and lawyer settin up shop with the lawyer servin as a doctor as the need might arise. Finally, folks had theirselves a town and they wanted to make the name of their home stand. It became Possum Crossing, Virginia, United States of America.

It stayed that way for quite a spell jest agrowin and prosperin. Until, that is, when things began to be a stirrin. The election of 1860 wuz quite an affair. There wuz Lincoln, and Douglas and Breckenridge and somebody else I'm not rememberin on. Anyhow, Lincoln wuz declared the winner and folks climbed the trees to see his election train pass by on the railroad on the Ohio side of the river. Jubal McCorkle, grandson of Noah, claimed he actually saw the new president as the train rolled by. Nobody ever challenged him, cause he wuz the best and fastest gun toter in Possum. You jest listened and nodded and figured it made no nevermind what he did or didn't see from that far away.

When the call came for troops to fight for the Union folks wuz ready to git in line and join up. The McCorkles weren't no 'ception. Jest bout all the boys, save for the youngins, stood at the head of the line. There wuz, however, one 'ception to which way the boys wuz to march. Paul said he couldn't fire no shots at fellow Virginians and so he made his way back east toward Richmond. The rest didn't have no love for easterners jest like Richmond had no love for the westerners. They marched out with the Union militia as Paul mounted old Betsy and headed east. Paul wuz never seen again in Possum. Some say he died a hero in some battle back east servin under the great Stonewall Jackson. If he did, no one ever recorded it for us to find. Most likely, the tale that he wuz captured and died in a prison camp wuz truer by far.

Anyhow, by the time the war ended we wuz no longer Possum Crossing, Virginia. Abe Lincoln had done made us a new state and we wuz now, Possum Crossing, <u>West</u> Virginia. It took town folks a while gittin used to that "WEST." Truth wuz we wuz might proud of bein on our own. It made more sense than bein under the thumb a Richmond. Our proudness got interrupted soon after the news of the war endin. No matter what side folks found a likin to, the shootin of the president wuz a sorry burden on their hearts. Hearts do a healin though and the town moved on from the shootin of Lincoln and the new "WEST" added to our name.

Not all returned from the war and some that did wuz not whole. Most wuz missin limbs and walkin with crutches tellin stories of the battles they had fought. Theodore McCorkle wuz one of them. He couldn't forget the war. All that he had seen kept comin back to him long after he returned. Story wuz that the boy standin next to him took a Minie to the head in the first battle Theodore saw. It was his best friend and childhood playmate, David Magilone, who had never fired a shot since joinin up and puttin on the uniform. Theodore had to brush the remants from his face and uniform afore he could advance with his company. He eased his mind by frequentin the local saloons that had blossomed on the main street in town. Drunk as a man could git on Saturday only to sober up and git saved at Sunday Mornin services. Them boys all knew that bad behavior wuz not a trait tolerated in a McCorkle. Have your fun but live like a Christian man is supposed to. That's what wuz expected in our Possum.

## Chapter II Growin and Prosperin

Possum continued to grow and prosper. It became a regular stop for the paddle-wheelers goin up or down river to Pittsburgh or Cincinnati. Goods wuz loaded and unloaded at the riverfront docks. Jest about anythin a man wanted came available right in town. However we had competition by then. The towns of Pone and New Hickory had sprung up and were growin fast jest like Possum. The railroad passed through New Hickory and started a boomlet of its own. Never could understand "New" Hickory and don't to this day. Where is "Old" Hickory or has it jest gone died of old age or somethin. All this growin and the bustlin economy put quite a strain on the County seat of Barletesville. Sides that, it was located way down yonder from our end of the county. Folks had to set aside three days for conductin business and travelin there. So the legislature did somethin smart for onest and divided the county of Lehigh in two. We became McCorkle County officially. New Hickory, Pone and Possum wuz in the runnin for the "honor" to be named the county seat. New Hickory finally got the honor bestowed on it and wuz named the county seat in a close contest. Heck, no real Possums wanted the danged thing anyhow. All them grimy politicians and lawyers millin about town and bringin their dirt and stink into beautiful Possum. Let them Hickory "sticks" have the dern county seat. The less time you spend within a stone's throw of a county courthouse the better in my way of thinkin.

What we did want though wuz the brick makin works started when J. Franklin Sidney came to town. Hired many a needful man to operate the ovens and work the mines. Yep, mines! Sidney said Possum had some of the best clay east of the mighty Mississippi. The McCorkle family sold the mineral rights under their farm and Sidney dug a spider web of tunnels right beneath the feet of the horses and cattle. They kept up their grazin as if nothin wuz happenin down under their very hooves. There wuz plenty goin on seein them mine shafts ran for over a mile under the farm. Nothin ever did happen to any critters even though townfolks said they expected to hear the cows drop down into them tunnels one day. Them bricks wuz in demand for all the buildin goin on in them big cities and Sidney wuz much obliged to accommodate them.

Wouldn't you know but that growin of the town drew K. Tolliver Cooper to open his "Cooper Iron Works and Fabrication." It had a mighty big need for lots of bricks for their ovens and bricks were there for the askin. Later, the name wuz changed to "Cooper Steel Works, Inc." It remained the largest employer in the county right up till recent time. Mr. Andrew Carnegie bought the mill eventually and it wuz thereafter folded into the United States Steel Company.

Time came when some places had a lot of strikin and fightin, and killin when the unions stepped in and certain folks got all fired up. There wuz some places the workers took over the mills and shut down the production. The situation wuz what you might call actual warfare over workin conditions and wages. All it took here in Possum wuz for a few Pinkertons to mosey on into town. Now a Possum ain't a dumb critter. When he sees he is surrounded and outgunned he don't start thumpin his chest and shoutin like a fool ape. Nope, he jest lies down and plays dead. That's what happened here in Possum. No one got killed, no one got hurt. Eventually they all made kissy face and said too bad about all the dead. All cept the dead, that is, they didn't say nothin. Guess a Possum is a darned smart animal!

The town folk kept showin up at the mines and the mill and the steel kept right on a comin. Bricks came pourin out like pancakes at the pancake flippin contest and the country needed all the steel we could make. Them "Newies" down in New Hickory had the courthouse and the law offices but we got the good un when we got that mill. Things wuz aboomin right on through the war years and Possum grew like a fat mellon on the garden vine. School kids said they didn't need no "edgecation" cause their Pa wuz goin to git them a job in the mill when they growed up. That there wuz pretty much fact right up to the 1960s when things started to change around town.

John F. Kennedy came to West Virginia and got hisself elected president of the United States. There was a tale around town that his brother Theodore brought a bag full of money when he came to visit the county Democratic chairman. A certain match missin from a matchbook certified you had done your duty and voted correctly on election day. It was right rewardin votin for Mr. Kennedy and lots of folks were willin to do it. He never visited Possum but we heard tell of all the news when he won the election in West Virginia and wuz on his way into history. A Roman Catholic in the White House and the country is goin straight to hell. At least that's what a few preachers had to say durin their mornin services. Most Possums paid little heed and jest went about their chores and shoppin. We ain't what you call big on all that political stuff. Most everyone in town is registered in the Democrats. My daddy said "I wuz born a Democrat and I vote Democrat and I ain't goin to vote for no Republican no way." We gave young Kennedy a good victory in the election and folks wuz purdy happy we done our part.

There wuz mighty big sorrow in town when we got the news JFK had been shot down in Texas. Everyone in Possum stayed close by the radio and TV to hear the news reports. Not a single copy of the Times wuz left for purchase anywhere in town. Everybody wuz buyin them newspapers up and puttin them away in cedar chests so they could share with their grandchildren. Turned out they wuz not as valuable as we expected since so many had saved them up. Years later, everyone said they could remember right where they wuz standin when the news done come. Business come to a total halt the day of the funeral. TV showed the whole thing and folks wuz a cryin for every last minute.

There wuz happier times later when we won the space race and got that Apollo rocket to the moon. Folks found it hard to imagine how a man could be standin there on the big ole moon. We had been watchin that ole feller risin up over the hills and settin down west over the river for as long as folks had been in Possum. Now there wuz Armstrong and Aldrin standin up there probably lookin down on us. Old man Wilkerson jest sat there in Duffy's Bar repeatin "amazin, amazin, moon men walkin about and not fallin off." He expected to see them drop off and fall back to earth. We tried esplainin how it wuz gravity that held them in place but he said "they rose up into the sky in that rocket. If you open the door in an aeroplane and step out, you'd hit the ground pretty durn quick. Seeins the moon is a tad higher in the sky you'd expect a day or so to come back." Matt Dobson, science teacher at the high school, tried again and again to make him understand about gravity but Wilkerson would tap his cane on the floor and say "what goes up must come down. Law of physics, taught by our physics teacher Miss Greer, and there ain't no changin them laws what the good Lord hath made." All them moon men stayed put on the moon so I guess them laws of physics must be a special case when it comes to moon men.

## Chapter III Slow Possum

In the seventies things began to git real slow in Possum. The mill cut back on the help till most of Possum wuz sittin at Maxi's coffee shop and talkin for better than half the daylight shift. We always got our fill with Maxi's bottomless cup and homemade donuts. Them donuts wuz the best gall dern donuts a man ever ate. You can't beat a hot donut with your mornin coffee and you can make that double for Maxi's donuts. Maxi wuz sellin almost as many as when the guys wuz workin at the plant. Best seller after breakfast wuz spaghetti and meatballs jest like always.

In the old days we'd order up a dozen or so platters and have them delivered to the plant gate. They came with plenty of garlic bread to go round and one of the guys made sure we had some locally brewed beer to wash it down. Now I never did, mind ya, but some wuz known to find a secluded spot to git some shut eye after a meal like that. Night turn wuz tough on a man's constitutional as is and jest got tougher after a man-sized plate of Maxi's best Eyetalian dish.

Pete O'Brien claimed once that he had more hours sleepin on the night shift than he had workin. All a count of that garlic bread he scarfed down. That guy could eat one whole loaf by hisself but insisted that it had amounted to but two slices when you consider that a loaf is cut in half lengthways. Garlic made him sleepy, he claimed, so sleepy he wuz forced to take a small nap. Same guy had the biggest feast in town at Thanksgiving. His wife, Mary Anne, wuz quite the cook and Pete let none of it go to waste. Spent the rest of the day on the sofa snoorin away. Turkey made him sleepy too. Must be made of the same ingredients as garlic. One thing that guy will never die from is lack of sleep. We even had trouble at huntin camp keepin him from dozin. "Ain't you afraid you'll miss a big buck while you're settin there with your eyes at ease?" Tom Stemple once asked him. "Nah, my rest is important and I figger I can take down the next two or three that wander on by." Always did somehow. Man had meat in the freezer all winter every year.

Possum has changed a lot since them days. Most of the stores downtown have long since closed. Lots of papered over windows and consignment shops all along Washington Street. Oh, we got the artsy craftsy stores that see little activity durin most of the week. Tween them and the antique stores folks have a lot of places to do a lot of "jest lookin, maam. Mighty fine goods you have here." A couple dollars spent here and there on rare occasions seemed to satisfy the storekeepers. They's jest what you might call a supplement to the family income.

Most everybody used up the unemployment checks long ago and either retired on social security or what pensions they could get. My case took the same route as everyone else cept I wuz only there a short time when they began cuttin back on jobs. Japan and Korea and China started gobblin up the steel production and us younger guys were left with unemployment. We wuz lucky in a way though considerin that the gov ment or "Uncle", as we like to say, eventually came by and offered us "disability." It wuzn't long afore jest about everybody in Possum wuz gittin a gov ment check of some sort. Only one man in my entire graduatin class of thirty-two is actually workin for a paycheck these days.

Clyde Randall wuz one of them proud Randall boys who refused to git on the gov ment bandwagon. Clyde always said his Papa taught him a man ought to work for his eats and he didn't reckon his Papa ever wuz wrong. He puts in his sixty hours a week at Simmon's scrap yard for minimum wage. Minimum wage, not a dime more; no benefits, no vacation days no chance for any wage increases. Rain or shine, you can drive by the yard and see old Clyde workin like he wuz gittin top dollar union wages.

At one point the gov ment started a "cash for clunkers" program. Now the clunkers wuz sposed to be crushed to smithereens. They got smashed all right, but not afore Wayne Simmons removed all the useable parts. You could git any part for any model car you wanted real cheap back then. Any smart feller could collect up them parts and figger out how to make hisself a pretty decent piece a transportation. I guess it wuzn't exactly accordin to the law but townsfolk never cared about that. Old Wayne wuz rollin in cash and he branched out to Pone and Newie onest he found the way to real riches.

Our country got into recyclin real big back then. Gov ment said us folks had to take care of the Viornment so we could save the planet. So we had bins for our metal, bins for our glass, and bins for our paper. Onest them bins wuz full they got taken to Wayne's place. Got paid a penny a pound for metal; nuthin for glass and paper. Wayne said they wuz a nuisance to mess with but he done it cause we had to save the

Viornment. Knowin Wayne I suppose he found a way to make hisself a dollar off the stuff. Anyway, the planet is still here rollin around the sun like always so I guess we took good care of the Viornment. Saved the planet we did; well at least I guess we did although I don't know how we did it. On the other hand, some experts say the planet is goin to git destroyed by climate change. Don't rightly see how that can be seein that the climate is always changin and I can't figger out how any man is goin to stop it. Maybe we done saved the planet jest so it could git destroyed. Gittin back to the story of Clyde:

Jim Baxter sez he sat down with Clyde one time and tried to show him the error of his ways. Jim put down with paper and pencil how it made no sense for a man to be wastin away like that when he could be settin with us at Maxi's. Clyde don't seem to be all that bright though. Jest keeps on a workin and gittin nowhere like he could be. No doubt the man's happy with his situation and will keep on workin till he can no longer. Jim says Clyde has the arthuritis and would qualify for disability in nothin flat. Clyde jest sez that's not what his pappy done told him.

Baxter hisself has what you can call a "bad back." Jim went to see a lawyer in New Hickory who got him on the gov ment benefits. Alls he had to do wuz go to a doc in Pone who certified he had a "bad back" and wuz unable to do a lick of work. Took some time and lots of doc visits afore the checks came through but Jim sez it wuz all worth it. Seems he got a few years worth of the benefits in a lump sum when he wuz all done gittin certified. Attorney Fitzhugh got a nice bit of the action too cause he knew all the ins and outs of gov ment red tape. Maybe that's why he drives a BENZ and lives in a mansion on the Hickory Heights. The Heights is where all them rich lawyers and doctors have their homes overlookin the Ohio River.

Attorney Ransom Fitzhugh don't do no other law cases. Disability is all he does. What you call a specialist. A dern good one if you ask me. I wished I would have gone to WVU and got me one of them law degrees. I weren't no good at books though and schoolin wuz not my better subject. I did what most did when school wuz over and went to work in the Worldwide Clay and Brick Works afore I finally lands me a job at the steel mill. Sidney had long ago sold out to a big corporate giant. First thing they did wuz change the name and bring in some big city manager types what knew the boss's daughter but nuthin about makin bricks. For a while at least I tried the old Clyde method of workin for my eats. It didn't last and the unemployment checks seemed a might easier than sweatin all day.

Don't you be a thinkin I'm a slacker though. Like I said, I tried the Clyde way but it jest don't seem to make sense to a thinkin man. I wuz entitled to them unemployment checks and when they ran out what wuz I to do? Possum wuz too nice a place to pack up and leave jest to git a job somewheres else. I had me a house, wife, spoiled rotten dawg and kids and you jest don't pack up and leave when somebody sez "Here's a check. Stay put and rest a spell. You is entitled to it."

## Chapter IV Fun Aplenty

I know what you must be thinkin by now; Possum sounds "BOOOOORINNG!" That's jest kinda what you big city folk like to say. It is 100% absolutely not true. Why, have you ever been to a Possum Volunteer Fire Department 4th of July parade with pumper #28 leadin the marchin band and all the fancy floats? They toss penny candy to all the youngins linin the streets. Some politicians, like state senator Dick Tost, ride in them convertibles and wave to the crowd all smilin and countin up the votes for the next election. What about the annual fireman's carnival? There ain't nothin like a corn dog, cotton candy and a wild ride on the Loop-O- Plane. You can even win a goldfish for the kids by tossin a ping-pong ball into the fishbowl. Goes on for a full week with lots of folk comin into Possum for the fun and thrills. There's farworks on the last nite and folks set on all the hillsides to git a better view of the display. All that boomin gits the dogs a howlin and runnin for cover. Always gits a lot of cheerin by the kids who usually run about shootin off firecrackers of their own. Talk about fun and it brings to mind the annual Christmas parade. Santa Claus hisself arrives aboard one of the volunteer fire department's fire trucks. He makes the rounds givin toys and candy at the homes of children who might find their Christmas gifts on the lean side otherwise. Possum has plenty of everyday year round entertainment for those who don't have cable TV or are unwillin to go out and enjoy huntin and fishin like a sensible man.

Why, there's bingo every Wednesday at the firemen's hall and the Cafés are open every day. We got thirteen of them right here in downtown Possum. Now you may not be familiar with the Café since you most likely play the Lotto or the scratch offs. The Café usually has four or so electronic gamin machines where you can strike it rich even on the penny machine. Don't git too excited bout that penny stuff. It will cost you about a quarter to garner in all those riches. Rob Newcomb's wife, Dottie, won $15,000.00 with one lucky pull on a machine down at Ruby's. Rob has always been a lucky guy. He takes his wife out west every year to try his luck at makin a fortune. Never has told folks how much these trips cost but they say he is what you call a high roller. Baxter says Rob has a "system" for makin those trips out and back for no cost to hisself. Somethin about the Salvation Army puttin them up wherever they might happen to land after hitchin for the day.

That "beep" you heard wuz Jim Baxter buzzin by and sayin "hey" out the window of his dazzlin purple Dodge Charger. Probably on his way over to Pone to pick up parts at the Auto Zone. That dude is always workin on them cars. He has five of them in the garage or back yard of his house. Likes to pull out the engines and do a replacement. Waste of time to me. Crawlin underneath them jacked up cars and liftin out the engines when they is runnin perfectly good as is. He's not much of a coffee drinker though so he gits bored at Maxi's. Jim wuz always the athletic type. Works out every other day at the YMCA. Still rides his ten-speed all the way to Pone and back three times a week. Not me, no siree! Twenty miles roundtrip; too many hills and curves on that highway. Don't like Pone much anyway. Nothin to do there. Folks in Pone feel the same way bout Possum.

Pone and Possum have been the fiercest rivals since I can remember. It's especially true in football. The Purple Possums like nothin better than to crush them sissy-pants bird-egg blue and gold Pone Panthers. Last year we smashed them 69 to 6. Would have been 72 if coach Burch hadn't substituted a freshman kicker for Tad Rollins. Tad hasn't missed a kick since he wuz in 7th grade. His dad made sure the boy wuz out there everyday practicin them kicks afore and after school. The kid knowed better than to miss again in a big game. One good kick in the ass taught him that he better not miss again. Yep, the Purple Possums are our pride and joy. Every fall nothin happens on Friday nites cept the BIG game. We pack the place for every home game. There's a whoopin and a hollerin after every team victory. Only thing better than that is a sound trouncin of Pitt by the West Virginia University 'eers. 'Eers is what we affectionately call the Mountaineers of WVU. Sandy's Ice Cream gives out free cones after every victory. Alls you pay for is the extry scoop if you want one and who wouldn't?

Two years ago the county wanted to merge the three schools into one for the entire county. They even tried to buy our votes by offerin to build a brand new million dollar sports complex with a fancy new Scoreboard and additional seats. Imagine wantin to put an end to the Purple Possums! No way that deal wuz goin down. The sissy-pants Pone Panthers didn't like the idea much either. The levy wuz defeated 72% to somethin or other. Anyhow the Purple Possums remained and

Pone and New Hickory kept their schools too. Only the nitwits in New Hickory thought it wuz a good idea. Lawyers wantin to make more money I suppose. You know there ain't much that escapes the sharpened claws of them lawyers. They smell the money all eighteen miles from Possum to New Hickory. You can ask Baxter; got his money only after the lawyer took his chunk of meat off the bones.

## Chapter V Lucky Dog

There goes Lori Sue Adkins drivin down toward the "Riverside Steak and Taters" in her new bright cherry red Chevy Impala. She goes down there several times every week to pick up Lulu's dinner. Lulu is her little "Chihula" dog. You know them little dogs from down Mexico way. They had them on the Taco Bell commercials a few years back. Anyhow Lulu is one lucky four legged critter in Possum. Lori Sue loves that dog like it wuz her child. Lori Sue ain't married or nothin and she don't have no kids. That makes her unusual for a single female in Possum. Most has a kid or two – or maybe three or four. They call them "single moms." That means they qualify for extry benefits from Uncle. They have that CHIP which covers their medical costs; course they also qualify for WIC program in addition to their welfare or SSI. Most of them has at least one boyfriend; usually they is alivin at the house or apartment and they has no marryin plans. Marryin results in losin them benefits they has acquired. Some folk have been livin "in sin", as the preachers say, for long enough to see their kids growed and with kids of their own. It's kinda passed down from generation to generation. The kids say when they is growed they wants to be on the welfare jest like mom and dad.

You should see them at Wal Mart down in New Hickory when the benefits come in. Most has two full carts of every kind of vittles you could dream about. I wuz behind a couple one day and they had eight cases of AquaFina bottled water. I didn't pay much attention to their other stuff since I wuz taken aback by all that bottled water. Never have been a fan of that

22

bottled stuff. Looks and tastes no better than our water from the tap to me. We done got the best tastin water in the entire United States of America here in Possum. Our water comes from an aquifer deep down below the Ohio River. They say it is an underground river called the Wisconsin which meanders on by unseen by man or beast. That there bottled stuff costs a whole lot more so I guess that's why they walk around town drinkin and a holdin them bottles for all to see. Lawrence Putnam got one of those discarded bottles out of the Frankie's dumpster onest. Filled it with eau de Possum and carried with him all about town. Said it made him feel real important to have bottled water.

Darned if I haven't strayed from my story about Lori Sue and Lulu. Well, seems Lulu is one of them real important type dogs. She got papers from the AKC which makes her a certified pure bred. She's a cute one, I'll be the first to admit to that. When that dog wuz a pup Lori Sue dressed her up like a little princess, tiara and all, and walked her in the middle of the Possum Volunteer Fire Department 4th of July parade. Kids wuz a squealin and folks wuz applaudin but the little "princess" kept her cool and strutted her stuff. Lulu won first prize in the small dog category and took first overall in the best Pup in Possum contest. Lori Sue treats her like a small child of her own.

Right now she's on her way over to the Riverside Steak and Tater restaurant to pick up Lulu's supper. Fillet mignon, medium rare, and loaded baked tater. Comes with a toss salad too but Lori Sue don't feed no "vegatation" to Lulu. Calls the order in for pick up pert neer every day and chef Dominic let it out to me that the meal's for Lulu. See, one time the fillet wuz too well done and Lori Sue burst out "Lulu ain't gonna like chewin this leather." Dominic said nobody else heard it so it should be kept from pryin ears if you know what I mean. Could be the gov ment is payin for the eats for that dog and I sure wouldn't want bet agin it.

Gittin back to Lori Sue, she sure is a real fine woman about town. Got the long blonde hair and a real nice figure to her. Eyes turn whenever she's in town. Lives out by Lake Gonetoofar on the other side of town. Folks named the lake when it became an easy way to give directions to the airport. If you got to the lake, you missed the turn off road and had "Gonetoofar." Afore that it wuz known as William T. Sherman Pond. Old William T. wuz our town blacksmith for many years. Course that were years ago. No need for one now. Horses have done been retired, not disabled, jest retired. When they painted the sign above his place ole man Jeff Brice painted: "Bill Sherman, Blacksmith." William T. saw that piece a artwork and he had him paint right over it. "Blacksmith and Livery. William T. Sherman, proprietor." Jeff wuz one that preferred to take a few shortcuts when he wuz a workin. Gave him more time to smoke his cigars and partake of a little medicinal shine.

Back to Lori Sue. She wuz one of the Adkins girls. Mary and Hank had eight children. Seven of them wuz girls. All cute and the marryin type; what with them nice figures. The boy joined up with the Marines and never came back from Nam. Girls have all done well, though. Lori Sue wuz workin for the Whinebush Home Healthcare from over in New Hickory. She done took care of ole man Rosenlieb when he had the old timer's disease. His Missus spent years lookin after him and finally kicked the bucket herself. Lori Sue worked at the house doin his chores and makin sure he took his medication. One day ole Rosenlieb went a bit crazy and thought she wuz the Missus. Nothin happened though. He wuz in a wheelchair and couldn't move too fast and Lori Sue had the 911 and police afore anythin commenced.

Poor Lori Sue couldn't work a day after that. She had the "scares" and couldn't leave her house. No worries, though, seems that means "disability." She's pretty much set these past seven years. Lives in a double wide mobile home with Lulu. Bein she is "disabled", she qualifies for property tax forgiveness. That there means she don't never pay no real estate property taxes. Gov ment has takin good care of her all this time. Two years ago they installed a new septic system for her. Didn't cost her a dime. Last year she got a new roof and well. That there outfit which done the work came to town from somewheres around Wheeling. The septic system alone cost $16,000.00. Lori Sue didn't have no worries though since she wuz due that as part of her benefits. Folks says the gov ment paid her bill but we all know the gov ment prints money but the earnin is done by us. That's not all of her benefits though, they transport her for medical treatments at no cost to her. Like I said she has the red Chevy Impala which she drives all the time. When it comes to the medical, though, she prefers the transportation van. It comes to her door and takes her to Wheeling to see the doc. Yep, Wheeling. She don't cotton to the docs in New Hickory and avoids the local hospital. Louie Maple's been drivin the van for years. Guess he jest sits there and waits hours till she's ready to come back to Possum. Even with the hourly pay rate what it is, Lori doesn't seem to mind the wait at all. Baxter sez it's a good use of the van since without Lori Sue's needs it would jest be sittin in the gov ment parkin lot gettin rusty. He brings her right back home to her door. I think she's on one of them medical programs so I don't guess the visits cost her a thin dime. No wonder she got no hankerin to marry.

Lori Sue done told this tale on herself. Onest she wanted to take a trip down to Bermuda. Nuthin says the "disabled" can't do no travelin, ya know. Well that "Chachinga" virus got to makin headlines and Lori Sue got to worryin about catchin it. She decided to go instead to a fancy hotel in Wheeling. Got the presidential suite, she did. Last occupant had been William Jefferson Clinton on one of his speakin engagements. She said it gave her chills all over sleepin in the same bed he done slept in. Never have been in a "suite" in my life. It don't look like I ever will.

Now you say to me how do you expect me to believe Lori Sue done did what you jest said. Well, Lori Sue applied for her benefits when she wuz "disabled." When they finally come, she is entitled to a nice chunk of cash. I don't pretend to know all the ins and outs of gov ment dealins but what she told me wuz the gov ment wuz supposed to keep a portion to be given out as her medical needs required. Kinda like an allowance you give a kid so he don't spend it all at onest.

Lori Sue told that administrator she needed all her money cause she never had a vacation and she felt she deserved one. They went back and forth recitin the rules and Lori Sue stood her ground. Finally, she come up with the idea of usin some "sweet talk" to try to convince the gov ment man. If you know Lori Sue you know she can pour it on thick as cream cheese on a bagel. She spread it on so thick he done give her the entire amount. When that girl butters up a gent, he is like hot fudge rollin over ice cream. Somehow he fixed up the paperwork and she done git her vacation paid for by Uncle.

Now I wouldn't want you to repeat what I'm about to tell you. There ain't no proof of it and I don't know what that any bit of it can be true. Jest so you know Possum like it is in reality I'm goin to relate this completely unverified tale of what I has heard folks tell. There's some talk about town, not started by me I reminds you, that Lori Sue has what you might call a personal business. There's menfolk here in Possum what has the arthuritis and the aches and pains which naturally comes with livin. They need to git some relief from these painful sufferins and it seems "massage therapy" can do a man a powerful lot of good. They say Lori Sue supplements her meager livin conditions with a offerin of "massage therapy" to the truly sufferin residents of the county. That, again, is totally unverified, unsubstantiated, and unreliable information. If anyone asks, I never told you any such tale and that be the end of it.

## Chapter VI Flying Possums

At the road on your right, jest afore Lake Gonetoofar, is the road to the county airport. Ah, airport you say, things must be pickin up in Possum. Not so, I tell you. That airport, located on a few acres of the Old McCorkle farm, wuz the idea of the county commissioners. Danny Weissmuller, the chief commissioner I guess you'd call him, convinced the other two commissioners that what McCorkle County needed to git back on track wuz an airport. "Redevelopment" they call it. We needed "redevelopment." There's funds available for "redevelopment" and if we didn't take them somebody else would step up and git the use of all them dollars. That "redevelopment" sounded real good to a lot of townfolk. We didn't have no airports in the county and Danny sayin the gov ment would pay most of the costs for construction through some sort of loan grant and that wuz enough to git folks to go along.

Don't bet against the commissioners when they have a project they want. The levy passed but jest barely so. It wuz quite popular with them lawyers in New Hickory and they talked it up real good. They had speedboats and fancy cars so an aeroplane sounded like a good next step. Sides, they could git to Charleston or Wheeling or wherever pretty dern quick. Danny got the county to purchase a Cessna 172 on account of we needed it to do aerial surveyin of the county. Originally it wuz "needed" so we could make our county up-to-date for the 911 information. We had a slight hiccup when we could find no one capable of flyin it in aerial surveyin.

They found a way to git the job done and that wuz a beaut of a project. The commissioners brought in Mid-Ohio Aerial Surveying and Assessment Corporation cause they had experience with this 911 identification work. Gittin this done wuz super urgent accordin to the commissioners. We had to git all mapped out and identified so we could be "in compliance." Now they didn't do all this mappin and surveyin in Ohio or Pennsylvania which is like next door neighbors. So we folks in Possum, McCorkle County, West Virginia are "in compliance" but them in Ohio and Pennsylvania are not. When is somebody goin to make them git "in compliance?"

At any rate Mid-Ohio came to town with a couple of them helicopters and several four-wheelers. Mid-Ohio made sure all streets had official names and posted signs to show townfolk what the street they lived on wuz called. A good many people in POSSUM already knew the name of the street they had lived on for all their lives. Now, however, they had a beautiful green and white sign which wuz put up by Rob Newcomb's Construction Company. Newcomb's always seems to git the low bid on any of these county buildin projects. Folks say Rob is pretty sharp when it comes to figgerin how to "undercut the competition" so to speak. We git them signs put up and made Possum look like an official first rate city. It surprised us though when Mid-Ohio informed us that our house numbers wuz wrong and they would assign the proper number.

Imagine wakin up one day and findin your house number 150 Lincoln Street wuz now 916. Those down at 925 wuz changed to 127. It made no sense to me so I called the county to git an esplanation. "Satellite. We got those numbers from the satellite. It knows better than you folks who have lived there for fifty years. You got to go by satellites these days. This is the space age. Git yourselves up to date with stuff. You are livin in the space age." So it wuz for three quarters of the year that UPS, USPS, Fire department and emergency ambulance wuz goin to the wrong location lookin for our houses which now had new numbers. They finally accepted the authority of the all knowin space satellite and went to the correct addresses. Didja ever try tellin your doctor or dentist that you got a new address for the records? "Oh, you and the Mrs. have moved, have ya?" Then you try esplainin that you is still in your same house where ya lived for fifty years but your address is different today from what it wuz yesterday. They give you puzzled looks until you esplain that it is the satellite what determined that you did not live where you live. Then they looks at you like you has jest escaped from a looney hospital. Onest they accept the facts you are tellin them, even if they don't understand what you has jest said, they is OK.

Gettin back to Danny again. He said the plane would make a great tool for the Sheriff to do searches for missin persons, lost dogs, bank robbers and escaped prisoners. It would also serve to watch for speeders through the county thereby increasin fees and producin work for the lawyers. Now I know that they has caught speeders galore since but I can't recall missin persons, bank robbers or escaped prisoners bein captured. It's tough to keep up with all these goins on I has to admit.

Haapo Markinen is the airport manager. Lot of folks figger he got the job cause he's married to Dorothy Weissmuller. That'd be Danny's sister. Anyhow, Markinen sets there most of the time jest playin checkers with Harvey Worthwile who is Danny's cousin. Harvey has the mechanics responsibilities. He gasses up the planes and directs them onto the runway for takeoffs. Sure seems a pilot ought to know which way to go since there ain't but one runway at the airport. Harvey says there could be fog or traffic which would make for unsafe operations. If there ain't but one or two planes a day it appears to me to be a sort of luxury. What do I know for Pete's sake? I ain't no mechanic or sophisticated lawyer.

The airport consists of a hanger for storin the planes and mechanical parts and the terminal buildin itself. A large green and white sign across the front proudly announces "McCorkle County WV Airport — Elevation 930 Feet." Below this is a digital clock with bright red numerals displayin the local time. This is for the benefit of those with no wristwatch, cell phone or other means of knowin the time. A smaller plaque lets the visitors know who wuz governor and who wuz county commissioners when the deed wuz done. You wouldn't want to go to no airport what didn't have the sense to tell you who wuz the county commissioners would ya?

Did I tell you that Markinen is known in town to have a high IQ and is super smart to boot? One time when I wuz out there waitin to see a plane land I got kinda tired waitin so

I went inside the terminal office as Markinen calls it. He's got a grey desk covered with dust cept where the checkerboard and his coffee mug sets. There's a couple chairs, telephone and a file cabinet of matchin color. He points to a chair and tells me to set a spell. Mostly wanted to chit chat to pass away some county time so to speak.

Twernt long afore we struck up some pretty serious conversation. I say that but to be honest I wuz mostly doin the listenin. Markinen wuz esplainin the Einstein theory of physics to me. He watches the Science channel on the TV the county provides for travelers. Yep, we have the very latest 60" LCD curved screen, surround sound, theater, cable TV to entertain air travelers in our airport facility. You can't expect people these days to go to a one horse airport without a TV to pass the time while waitin. Anyhow, Markinen commences tellin me about physics theory. I found out we live in a universe which is extremely immense but what came from a tiny speck which is so small you can't even see it even with the most powerful microscope invented by man. You call that speck a singalarity which takes up no space at all. So somehow all the stars and us, and other stuff got crammed and squoze into that teeny tiny space you can't even see and neither has anyone else. You can't see it but them equations says positively it's there and you had better believe it cause they done told you so.

Haapo amazed me even further when he told me about the Shottentot's cat. Seems that there Herr Shottentot figgered out that if you put a cat in a box he could be alive or dead. That didn't impress me too much since I've seen plenty of livin and dead cats around Possum through the years. What he said next floored me like a junk car droppin from the magnet at Simmon's trash yard. The Shottentot's cat is a special case causin Herr Shottentot figured out that the cat wuz alive and dead at the same time. Now I heard the most profoundest thing I done ever heard. A dead cat that wuz alive and a livin cat that wuz dead. Markinen says all you need to do is to put the cat in the box and ask yourself what is the cat? Alive? Dead? He could be either one since you can't see a cat with a box over it. Least ways not if it ain't meowin or nothin. I guess this Shottentot musta assumed that his cat wuz one of them quiet ones or else it wuz sleepin when he put it in the box. So's this noiseless cat is settin there in the box, not movin around else you would hear him/her scratchin around. Shottentot didn't say if it were a girl cat or a boy cat. Really, wouldn't matter t'all what sex or color the cat wuz. Course he had to be livin when you put him in or else he would be dead. But if you put a dead cat into the box it would come back to life. Otherwise it couldn't be both alive and dead at the same time.

This Shottentot missed his callin. He should have been an undertaker. Let's say you put dead people in a box and tells the astonished family the dearly departed is alive inside that box!

Imagine the money ole Dyke Taylor down at Taylor's Funeral Home could make usin this scheme. "Yes, maam, I can tell you that it is a scientific fact proven by Herr Shottentot that the dearly departed is now alive and dead at the same time. Seein that our dearly departed may be livin, you most assuredly would want to place him/her in the finest **casket** we have here available. No way would you want to place them departed in a cheap pine **box** when they may be livin inside for who knows how long the universe will last. This here mahogany model would be much more appropriate for our dearly departed soul. Or what about this exquisite chestnut inlaid model with solid gold accents?" Shazam! The weepin, grief stricken widow looks on in amazement and gladly hands over her check for the full amount (no discount requested for this type of service). I can see $ signs in my eyes when I gits a commission for every funeral when I can esplain this here Shottentot cat paradox to Dyke. Not only that but I could franchise this idea. We could go all over the country. I can see myself sittin on a beach ticklin my toes in the surf and sippin a pina colada. Livin the life of the rich and famous; rubbin elbows with billionaires. My future secure because of a dead cat. Markinen, failin to observe such phenomenon as the trance I had fallen into, wuz back mutterin about black holes which is not really holes but a whole bunch of stuff squoze into a thing nobody has ever seen. Since you can't see 'em they has got to be black on account a space is black except where there is light or somethin like that.

Haapo and Dorothy and the kids are all church goin members of the West Monroe Street Church of the Nazarene. We knows them better as Nazarenes. Well Haapo stops me dead in mid question when he confides in me that he is really an atheist. He's the first one of them I ever met. I mean you don't see too many folk here in Possum what claims they is atheists. Be that as it may, I listen intently as he esplains how his daughter Audrey came back from her schoolin at WVU and told him how her professor said we all came from nothin. It seems a zillion trillion years ago every person, animal, plant, dog, cat, fish, stars and whatever wuz squoze into the singalarity he talked about. Audrey says they don't believe in God there because it weren't nobody around when the singalarity exploded and made everythin jest as it is. Haapo said she didn't learn how all that stuff got squoze into the singalarity or who wuz doin the squozin. Seems like a might important question to me. Markinen says you ain't supposed to ask what wuz afore the singalarity because we don't have no scientific equations for that.

Now gittin back to the black hole, we do have lots of equations for that. You can git close to a black hole but you can't see inside it even if you got close enough to fall in the hole. If'n you did manage to fall in you would be spaghettified. In other words the thing turns everythin into spaghetti; he didn't say if it wuz whole wheat or gluten free or whatever. In any case, everythin gits torn to pieces and you have some sort of spaghetti which is soup-like ingredients. They can't never git out and we can never see them. Jest like that cat in the box nobody knows nothin about them that went inside. He says they could come out in another universe if they go through a wormhole. Now that done blows my mind! What the heck would you want to come out into another universe after you are turned into spaghetti? What if there is Eyetalians there with marinara sauce and meatballs jest waitin for you to appear? Why would you want to go through all that jest so someone could twirl you around their fork and send you down the hatch? These here scientists can't believe God exists but they swallow all this spaghettifin stuff. It gits even worse.

Markinen told me there is collapsed stars out there where a teaspoon full of them would weigh as much as a mountain. Pulsars is what astronomy people call the dern things. These shoot out x-rays what would kill anythin in their path. What good is such a thing? Seems to me we ought to shoot up a rocket with an atomic bomb to blow those things to bits before they shoot them rays at us. Scientists are always findin out things what done makes no difference to a common man. You take them photons which come here from some star a billion, trillion light years away. They knows when they leave the star where they is supposed to land up. Now, either them photons are the smartest things in the universe or someone is guidin them like little race cars on a track. They say the Milky Way galaxy is goin to collide someday with another galaxy and we are goin to be destroyed. If that be true, why are we botherin to save a planet set for destruction we are powerless to stop?

You also can have a white hole which isn't a hole either. It's jest the opposite of a black one like black and white are opposites. Einstein figgered all this out usin equations jest like we had in math class. If Mr. Arturo Funkenbush, my math teacher, had told me the importance of those algebra equations I would have learned a lot harder so I could understand the universe like Einstein. Markinen would have gone on longer but he said he had some important airport paperwork to attend to and sides that wuz enough for one day's lesson. I want to go back out there someday so I can git better learnin on space and atoms in the universe of emptiness which is not really empty since it contains black matter and black energy. I'll have to ask him next time about where is the white matter and white energy. Why don't we have purple matter or blue or green matter? How come these here scientists don't like technicolor like in the movies? It is apparent that I missed my callin by not becomin a world famous scientist like Einstein or Herr Schottentot.

Markinen shuffles his papers and I git myself in gear and leave. Onest outside the entrance, I saw Sheriff Thatcher's blue & gold & white Cessna parked inside the hangar. His name wuz emblazoned on the sides with a big "Sheriff" sign and badge to make it easily identifiable. At least it would be easy to recognize while it wuz on the ground; in the air it's jest another plane. They usually puts it on a trailer and pulls it behind his big "Sheriff" car durin the 4th of July parade. Jest in case anyone forgot his name he parades the "Sheriff Thatcher" car and plane for those interested in knowin the name of their sheriff.

These officials likes to have their names afore the public as much as possible. Jest over the state line on Route 8 sits a big "Welcome to Wild and Wonderful West Virginia" sign. They got a scene with mountains and deer and a river runnin through it and then "Billie James Hoggsfeet, Governor." I don't know why all these visitors to our state want to know the name of our governor. Never once do I recall anyone askin me the governor's name. They stop and ask directions; where an eatin place is located; where to find the address of some friend but never do they say "would Billie James Hoggsfeet happen to be your governor?"

Sheriff Thatcher put up a smaller sign next to the official state sign statin "Don Thatcher, Sheriff." Folks don't ask about the sheriff either, but perhaps they stopped and stared at the beauty of the sign. Maybe they wuz admirin the fine printin or somethin.

Now gittin back to that plane, it wuz a standin there all polished and shiny. Sheriff Thatcher's #1 deputy Travis J. Dawgg wuz keepin a sharp eye to it so maybe some thief had plans to abscond with the thing. Travis does a lot of investigatin and special assignments for the sheriff. Townsfolk refer to Travis as deputy Dawgg but not to his face.

You got to be careful around Travis. He's the main reason Sheriff Thatcher is sittin in office today. A former deputy by the name of Bud Anderson decided to run against Thatcher in the election. Suddenly someone "discovered" Anderson had been too aggressive when arrestin a very intoxicated man. They even brought the Feds in to remove Bud as a threat to Thatcher by chargin him with violatin the drunk's civil rights. Imagine that, a drunk endagerin lives on the highway and pickin a fight with a state trooper and a deputy sheriff is treated better than us regular folks. Of course, Travis bein Thatcher's right hand man wuz more than willin to testify for the gov ment. It jest wouldn't do for a sheriff settin pretty as a toad on a lily pad to have opposition when he wants to be re-elected.

These charges wuz brung more than a year after the incident in which Travis and the state trooper wuz unable to subdue the drunken man in a terrific fight. That drunk wuz able to lift Travis clean over his head and almost tossed him over a guard rail. The trooper and Travis wuz overpowered by a drunk with "super human strength." Deputy Anderson arrived on the scene and the drunk had met his match. Wuzn't long till Bud had the bum handcuffed and tossed into the deputy's car. Bud ain't no weaklin like some of these dudes totin stars on their chests.

At any rate, the video of the affair wuz "lost" when Travis let a month go by without downloadin it. Mighty convenient when you wish to besmirch the character of a deputy who has served faithfully on the force and whose real "crime" is his challenge of Thatcher. Everyone said the whole thing smelled to high heaven cause the big name prosecutor from Wheeling and the sheriff wuz closer than a tick on a dog. No matter that experts testified in court that Anderson had acted properly as a deputy were taught. If you got that respected Eyeflounder family name and the FBI behind you the jury is like clay in your hands. Officially, of course, Thatcher claimed he had nuthin to do with the case. Seems all this paperwork and federal charges wuz done without tellin Thatcher a thing that wuz goin on in his very own sheriff's department. Why, he couldn't have known a thing about FBI agents questionin his deputies. Yep, and I own a bridge in Brooklyn I can sell ya real cheap!

Anyhow, Travis wuz givin me the evil eye when I approached the plane and dared to place my hand on the fuselage. "Keep your mitts off county property. Don't you know you're placin finger prints which might confuse a future investigation?"

I jumped back and jerked my hand away. "I wuz jest admirin this here fine vehicle the Sheriff has acquired," I muttered meekly.

"Do your admirin from a five foot distance so's you don't interfere with the delicate operational equipment. And don't call it no vehicle seein it's a investigational tool." Deputy Dawgg had his hand on the holster like he wuz gittin ready to draw the weapon. I figgered it wuz best to do my admirin of one of the other planes parked outside.

Jest about that time Markinen appeared from around the corner. "Mornin, deputy. Glad to see you here on the job lookin out after the county property." Dawgg grinned broadly and resembled a fattened hog ready for the roast. He still had his hand holdin onto that gun. I commenced to walkin further away from the area. Markinen wuz at my heels talkin about how the county's money wuz bein well spent. Not wantin to git either Markinen or Dawgg riled up, I nodded and muttered "makes a man right proud, yes sir."

'Bout that time we meet up with Worthwile wipin some grease off his hands. Markinen pipes up, "Say, Harv, why don't you take our friend here on a tour of the airport facilities? He's one of them taxpayers who pays for it. Give him a nice show."

Worthwile kept on wipin those hands and nodded ever so sheepishly. His grey coveralls were pretty well worn and covered with dirt. The county may have issued them but they wuzn't goin to do a man's laundry for him. "Come on, let me show you the inner workins of this fine facility." With that he leads me away from the front of the open hangar door and round toward the back. "This here is our trash disposal and recycle area," he says pointin to a couple of dark green dumpsters which had the look of a little wear and tear. "The commissioners bein aware of the need to keep the planet clean for future Possums...and Pones and Newies has instituted a policy of strict recycle. This here's our trash bin," pointin to the first dumpster. "We try our best to keep this here trash what can't be used for anythin to a minimum. Now here you have the actual recycle divided containment by categories thing-a-magig. Danny came up with this money savin idea whereby we use one containment which is divided into glass, metal and paper categories."

"Looks like a dumpster with two dividers in it to me, Harv" I replied.

"Oh no, this is a real money saver for the county. All these recycles goes to the scrap yard and gits turned into green cash. That's why we call it 'THINK GREEN. RECYCLE'."

That fancy dumpster had one of them recycle symbols on the outside of it along with the names of all three county commissioners. Danny is always thinkin of ways to keep his name afore the public eye.

We walk alongside of the terminal buildin which Harv is esplainin is the terminal buildin. "That's where Markinen has his office," he points out rather matter of factly. "Now, as you can observe, the other half of the terminal buildin is at the moment unfinished. That's where the restaurant is planned to go."

"Restaurant?" I question rather loudly. "Well, not right away, of course. That's future buildin plans. Right now we use the coffee pot and microwave in Markinen's office. He has a small fridge behind his desk. There's also a vendo machine in the main part of the terminal for any visitors. Plenty of good eats available at reasonable prices which profits the county immensely. Right over here is the buildin for the pilots and flight school. Tim Pickens has his trainin room for student pilots in there."

Sure enough there wuz a big blue and white sign sayin 'Pickens Aviation and Flight School. Tim Pickens, Gen. Mgr. & Instructor."

We went behind the main buildin to head back toward the parkin area. "What the **** is that, Harv," I says pointin to a yellow plane planted nose down into the ground. The wings were within touchin distance of a man standin underneath.

"That's one we planted in the spring. Not full growed yet. Hope to pluck her out in October when she's full ripe," he says gigglin and a laughin to hisself. "Nah, Danny's boy, Justin, flipped that one on his first lesson from Tim. Lucky as a kid on Christmas; he jest missed clippin the main buildin. He wuz plannin to git his license and go to work for the county as chief pilot. He'd be on duty 24/7 to look for bad guys, escapees, and the like. Sheriff's department wuz payin full price for them lessons and trainin. Pickens wuz sure upset about it. Mad as hell. Swore up and down and so loud he musta been heard in downtown Possum."

"Danny came out pretty dern quick and calmed things down afore the kid got tore to shreds and fed to the lions for lunch," Harv continues. "He went into Pickens' office and set quite a spell. When they came out theys all smiles and Danny wuz pattin Tim on the back. Shortly thereafter Tim got the contract to fly the sheriff's deputies to Charleston when they need to git their trainin."

"Looks like they ought to git that plane out of the ground and repaired so's they could git it flyin again," I wondered out loud.

"Nah, Pickens got the insurance money and Danny thought it'd be a attraction to git lots of attention. Folks like you always say 'Gee, gosh darn wallekers, what happen there?' Well, I got to git back to work. Judge DiPetro is due in this afternoon. He's got the big twin engine job. Sounds real loud when he taxis up to the hangar. I got to give him A Number One attention. I've been on probation since the wife and I had that little disagreement. Them bruises is gone but her broke arm ain't quite healed allt the way. See ya later, eh?"

## Chapter VII Errands and Stuff

I walked back to my truck in the parkin area in amazement. I say 'parkin area' cause it ain't no parkin lot what is all paved and lighted. It has them white lines on the grass and numbered meters at each space. Costs a quarter to park unless you intend to remain all day. "All day Parkers should report to the terminal buildin for permit," the sign over the entrance road announces. Once again there is the names of the commissioners jest in case you have forgotten. I done put my quarter in the meter knowin this wuz goin to be a shorter stay. Sides, I know Markinen wuz checkin the meter when I wuz tourin with Harv. I spied him glancin at my meter when we wuz admirin the recycle area.

Since it wuz past noon it wuz too late to make my stop at the bank. The Northern McCorkle Bank and Trust Company, which folks here calls the Norkle, closes early on Wednesdays. 'cept if you is willin to go through the drive-in spots. Lots of people in Possum use these here ATMs to transact their business. I realize the bank would like to have everyone switch to the ATMs and have automatic deposits of their checks and automatic bill payin. Everythins electronics. No need to have any cash money in your pocket; you jest flashes the magic card or taps a few keys on a computer and quick as a flash your money is gone. You don't actually see it go anywhere. You can't see it go because it don't never move.

Burt MacTavish is the manager of the local branch of the Norkle. He esplained to me that practically no cash ever goes anywhere. The bank sends a electronic signal that tells another computer that Tom Jones, for instance, jest sent his entire earnings to The Potowanime Electric Company. Now Tom has zero dollars left in his account and someone else has Tom's money. Looks like to me anyone with the proper knowledge and brain smarts could decide to transfer Tom's money. Say some guy in California wuz in need of a few extra dollars to pay his supplier or some Russians wanted to git rich grabbin money from Americans like Tom; then all they need is the little signal and it's bye-bye bank account cash.

Don't think of it that way Burt assures me. You are protected by the federal gov ment against any loss by such fraud and deceitful tactics. Now that there sets me a worryin real bad. A guy workin for the federal gov ment is a settin there in Washington, DC and watchin all those zillions of electrical blips and he is goin to give my blip special attention so that it don't git hijacked by some computer hacker. That there makes as much sense to me as believin lilacs will be bloomin through the snow in January.

Burt is a real good guy though. He'd do about anythin to help you out at the Norkle. Tries real hard to sign people up for all this modern electronic stuff but I ain't a buyin it. Seems everytime I go to the teller (the real live person, not the machine one) for a transaction they asks me if I'd be interested in obtainin one of these ATM cards or how about "our no fee VISA card? You can use it practically anywhere jest like cash." Why would I WANT THE DANG THING IF IT IS jest LIKE CASH? I have cash in my pocket right this very minute; Washingtons, Lincolns, Hamiltons and Jacksons. That there Jacksons is one I use up pretty quick. Somethin about that man I never did like.

So I tries to keep my regulars on my person. Onest in a while I git a Franklin in my envelope. Them things are the first to go. Prices bein what they are you can't have ole Ben in your pocket for very long.

Nah, nice as Burt is, I can't git my wagon hitched to these electronic gizmos. It's nothin personal. I jest likes the natural way of doin things. Take when I need a loan. I raps on Burt's office door and says "excuse me Mr. MacTavish but have you got a minute?" "It's 'Burt' and I got all the time you need. What may I do to be of assistance to you? Have a seat, have a seat." We set there a spell talkin about Possum and how it has changed since we both growed up. Lots of memories of times better than today. It ain't like them big city banks.

Burt got appointed general manager of the Possum branch of the Norkle by Judge DiPetro who is the founder and chief stockholder of the bank. He picked a real good man, yes siree. MacTavish knows everybody in town. Knowed them since they wuz little kids. Knows every family and which ones is good for credit. Bob Scott, the former manager, wuz a little too loose with the loan makin. The Norkle had plenty of bad loans on the books when MacTavish took over. Scott wanted to impress DiPetro with all the approvals of car loans for the DiPetro Central McCorkle Motor Car Company. Sold lots of them cars but folks thought they only had to make them car payments when they wuz in the mood. Now if you have hundreds of car loans which is months late on their payments the bank is losin money big time.

Wuzn't long afore MacTavish picked up the phone and told folks they had better git down to the bank with the payments. Some folks said "well you can jest take the dang thing back." They didn't realize they wuz bein held to the full amount of the loan. A few folks thought they could jest ignore these requests for payment and keep the car hid out so they couldn't be repoed. Burt wuz pretty smart about where they wuz hidin them cars and one by one he had the Repo man go git them cars in the middle of the night. It pays to have an intimate knowledge about the folks you is dealin with. Some came into the bank demandin the return of their vehicle. Burt jest esplained to them hows they could git it back when they got their payments up to date. Darned if most of them didn't reach into their wallets and pulled out the cash. Money jest kept on flowin back into the bank.

That ain't all Burt done for the Norkle. Onest there wuz a dude from out of town who came into the bank thinkin it wuz a good target for a robbery seein it wuz a small town bank without much local police protection. Handed a note to the teller sayin "give me the cash drawer in this bag." He took off for the door with the bills aflyin everywhere. Burt came out of his office and wuz right on the tail of the robber. The getaway driver seein this took off leavin his pal behind. The guy with the cash started runnin through town with Burt right on his heels. Burt would have caught him too but the dude turned around and pointed a gun and fired a shot. Lucky for Burt the bullet missed his head by inches and struck a cement block wall nearby. Burt figured he best fall back and give a little distance. Bout that time the Sheriff's cars started arrivin on scene.

There wuz deputy cars everywhere. They pulled out automatic rifles and ordered folks to stay inside and lock their doors. Deputies had been delayed from respondin to the alarm cause the robber had set off fireworks and bottles of gasoline on the highway leadin into Possum. The volunteer fire department put out the fires and that sent deputy sheriff cars racin to town. They brought out the K-9s and wuz searchin everywhere. Somehow the dude managed to evade capture but his getaway driver wuzn't so lucky. The cops chased him down and took him into custody thanks to the vehicle description Burt gave them. The Sheriff's plane got into the air searchin for the other robber but didn't spot nothin. Some folks think he jumped into the river and swam back to Ohio. Deputies managed to git the getaway driver to give up the name of the shootin bandit and the case wuz closed. Never did hear how much money wuz taken and if they recovered the cash. Some of it wuz alayin all about town and folks wuz pickin up $$$ jest like candy at the 4th of July parade. That wuz one of the most excitin days in Possum in quite a while.

Burt ain't one lookin for no publicity or platitudes from the admirin public so he didn't talk much about his participation in the search. The FBI wuz called in on the case which wuz quite pleasin to the sheriff. Got his picture on the front page of the local paper posin with them FBI investigators. The Norkle wuz showed there too so folks could see what the doors of the bank looked like. It wuz the talk of the town for quite a spell.

Speakin of the paper, you should know that Burt MacTavish's wife, Tamra, is the editor of THE MCCORKLE TIMES. It wuzn't always called the TIMES though. Back in 1847 Thaddeus P. Prendergast came to Possum and started up our first real newspaper. Named it the Possum Press of McCorkle County. Old Thaddeus wuz in the forefront of the abolitionist movement and made no bones about it. He pushed hard editorializin when Abe Lincoln wuz arunnin and got up front with the folks pushin for separation from old Virginie. Folks in the western counties never wuz too happy with Richmond so it seemed natural that we should be our own state.

Guns wuz ablazin and folks wuz whoopin all through town when it came down that Uncle Abe wuz finally goin to set us free. Bonfires wuz lit down by the river and we showed them Ohio folks that they wuz not the only state west of the mountains. There wuz politics about where the capitol would be but that didn't concern us since Possum wuz never in the runnin.

Thaddeus ran that paper till his death in 1883. Never any doubt where he stood on any issue of the day. Prendergast had strong opinions and wuz not afraid to put it out there for all to read. The kids took over the paper with his eldest son Matthew in charge of editorial opinion when the old man croaked. The name of the paper wuz later changed to THE POSSUM PRESS. It circulated all through the county jest like when Thaddeus wuz in charge. Matthew had strong views like his Pa and they sort of took the Republican side of politics. It stayed in the family until the 1960's when none of the kids or grandkids took much interest in it. They up and sold out to a big conglomerate, the Ogilvie Publishing Corporation of Wheeling.

Olgilvie built a new buildin and press room for the paper and changed the name to THE MCCORKLE COUNTY TIMES. Townfolks here in Possum wuz told they wanted to have greater appeal in Pone and New Hickory. It wuz that way for a few years when they decided to shorten the name to THE MCCORKLE TIMES. Everyone knew it wuz a county anyhow so it made no big difference to us. Might be they jest wanted to save on ink. You know how them big time accountants is always scratchin and figgerin how to cut costs.

Tamra MacTavish wuz put in charge a while back and she started makin some changes of her own. She tried to run more local stories especially involvin the local high school sports teams. Yep, she done a lot to keep our local paper goin strong. The fall edition with pictures of the entire Purple Possum football team lined up there in front of the football field is a real winner every year. Got schedules and last year's scores. There's stories on players the coaches is countin on this season. Local merchants sponsor a contest to pick the winner of each week's games. Man, the town is proud of the Purple Possums.

Right now I'm apassin the fork in the road that runs up to Alfie Parquette's cabin. Alfie is better known to townsfolk as "The Hermit". After Alfie came back from Nam he wuz feted as a war hero by the townfolk. Parades and marchin bands and lots of hoopla. Alfie Parquette had medals all over his chest and we wuz real proud of him. Weren't no name callin or spittin like in them big cities. No, we done had ourselves a real hero and folks wuz right proud to call him a Possum. Afore he joined up he had been the captain of our Purple Possums that year. It wuz like gittin a double dip of ice cream at Sandy's on a Friday nite after football.

Alfie smiled some and thanked folks, shook a lot of hands, and then sort of wandered off by hisself. Built a log cabin out at the end of Fishhook Road and didn't come to town much after that. He came in around sunset and loaded up on supplies and then toted them back out the cabin, sayin little other than what supplies he would be a needin. After a few years folks stopped callin him Alfie and jest said "The Hermit". Talk has it that he communicates with them animals out there. Lives with no electricity, no runnin water cept for the stream passin by and no indoor plumbin. Heats the cabin with wood he chops all summer and does a lot of readin since he ain't got no cable TV.

Ever so often some people from Possum takes up some staples and drops them off at his place. Never see him when they's out there but the goods always disappear after they've been left for him. Some folks say he done gone plum crazy after seein all the killin and maimin in the war. I think he jest got tired of all the craziness he saw when he come back home. Anyhow, now he likes bein out there in the woods with the animals more than bein with all them humans. The high school boys in town like to take their girls out to the cabin when they wants to give them a good fright. It's all spooky out there after midnite and the girls git pretty shook up thinkin that hermit is goin to git them if they don't stay real close to their boyfriends. Nobody has ever seen the hermit on these excursins but there is plenty of bloomers left along the road. I'm sure the hermit puts them to some kinda use since he keeps his area pretty pristine.

Onest I git back to town I see Missy Manford walkin toward the drugstore. She got the kids in tow walkin right behind her. There's Mandy, Marilyn, Maybelle, Marsha, Meadow, and Mayflower holdin hands with little Mikey. There's no sign of Muscle, her husband of sorts. His real name is Mikel Montcreif Manford but folks jest calls him Muscle since he is always workin out buildin his muscles. When he ain't workin out he pays a lot of attention to Missy. Sherry, over at Sandy's Ice Cream, says Muscle came there with Missy on their first date. He bought a triple dip cone for hisself; didn't offer to git anythin for Missy. But anyways she had them goo-goo eyes and didn't seem to care. After, they continued the walk down the street. Missy jest held his hand while he continued to eat that big ice cream cone. He thinks of hisself as "Mr. Romance" who is desired by all the cute girls in town.

Muscle don't have no job workin since he's disabled. Been that way since shortly after graduatin high school and workin for a while at the scrap yard. He quit after five months cause he claimed to have a bad back. Went to see Attorney Fitzhugh and got hisself certified for the disability payments. He's done collected more in disability than he ever made workin. They had but the one kid, Mandy, when he started on them payments. Jim Baxter says he's entitled to more money now that the other kids has managed to git birthed. If times git any rougher I expect to see Missy sportin another pair of pregnant bloomers. A man gits pretty tuckered out liftin all them weights so I figger he needs to git a bit of relaxin when he gits back home. Baxter once told me that Muscle could out lift any man in the county if it came down to a contest.

I don't go over to the Wal Mart in New Hickory around the first of the month. That place is jest too crowded to fight your way past the shoppin carts and those gall darn motor carts. Folks is a whizzin around corners in them dern things and is threatenin to smack you down. They ought to require a safety course for them drivers or maybe a license. You see a lot of disabled people heavy enough to outweigh the vehicle they is drivin. Some of them waddle up to the machines and plop down like a hippo squattin in a mud puddle. They sets on the cart with a good bit of flesh hangin on all sides. Must take all the power the motor can put out to git them movin. Maybe all that poundage is hard to control onest it gits movin because they sure have trouble gittin them to stop when they is headed right towards you. A lot of them has those oxygen tubes up their noses and them blue tooths in their ears. You see quite a few talkin on their cell phones and not payin much attention to whereabout they is goin.

Speakin of cell phone, I don't have one. Why on earth would I want to carry a phone around so's people could be acallin me all hours of the day and night? If I had one, the wife would be callin all the time askin me to pick up this or that and the kids would be callin sayin they needed money for gas, or money for Huggies, or bailin them out when they got into trouble with the law. Nope, I ain't never goin to be tied down to some dern electronic device which keeps tabs on me and makes me subjected to the beckon call of every dern tootin soul which wants to communicate with me.

Did you ever watch these cell phonies? They is drivin along talkin and not payin attention to their drivin. Saw many a crash where they wuz too busy talkin about nothin. And do you know they use them devil devices for somethin called 'texting'? Instead of jest talkin to another person they use the gall dern things to type out messages to each other. Why onest I seen a young couple settin at a table next to ours over at the Riverside Steak and Tater. Nice lookin couple. Neatly dressed and not yet ready for marryin. Jest out for a nice meal and some good times. They weren't sayin a word to each other. After the waitress took their order they smiled at each other like they wuz about to exchange a smooch over the table. Nope, they took out their cell phones and started textin. One would tap in a message; must have been a joke cause the other commenced laughin. Then the other would reply by textin also. They kept this up even after the waitress brought their meal. They would take a few bites and then commence more textin again. Never spoke a word. Waitress comes and he pays the bill and the two of them walk out after never havin spoken a word. Not a single, solitary syllable came out their mouths. Great date!

Like I said, I got no use for them gadgets. Practically everyone in town has one though. I even seen Wally Mugford walkin downtown talkin on one of them things. Wally is so poor I couldn't figger how he could afford one of them things.

"Whatcha doin talkin on the infernal gadget," I said to him rather rudely.

"Oh, this ain't no talkin cell phone" Wally says. "I found this here thing in the dumpster at Frankies."

Now afore I git any further you gotta understan that Frankies is the only supermarket of sorts in Possum. It's the old fashion grocery store type where you have only four checkouts and not one is the automatic electronic type. Clerks look at the price tag and ring up the item on the register. They don't have no way to read them "jail bar" codes on the packages. The management at Frankies says it can't afford the cost of installin those expensive automatic checkouts. A lot of folks is glad these old fashioned places still exists; it's comfortin to hold on to part of the past. They have a dumpster in back for store trash and a lot of townsfolk goin by decide to "borrow" the use of it.

"I brushed it off and started pretendin I had a lot of important calls to make. It doesn't work anyhow. I jest wants folks to think I'm conductin important business. It kinda gives me status here in town."

"You mean you're walkin around holdin the gall dern device to your ear and speakin into somethin that isn't even workin?"

"Looks good don't it? Sometimes I flip my finger around the screen so folks will think I'm usin some apps," he replied.

Now if that don't beat all. Maybe I should git a used one that doesn't work so folks'll think I'm important too. That'll be the day! I wuz beginnin to feel a bit hungry and thought I would go into the burger joint and pick up some lunch. I git me a cheeseburger, fries and a extra large coke. I git extra large jest as a sort of protest to the nitwits in New York City where they don't allow you to buy one. Ha, I feel pretty good holdin that extra large drink in my hand. "Come on, you Yankees, try to pry this drink from my constitutionally protected hands. I triple dog dare you to try it."

Possum Park is where I'm headin with my grub. It is real nice little park where you can have a bit of privacy if you wish. When I come to the entrance I am greeted with a large green and white sign statin "WELCOME TO POSSUM PARK. HELP KEEP THE PARK CLEAN. STASH YOUR TRASH."

Fine, I got no problem with that. I like places that are clean. What I do have a problem with is the rest of the sign. "Enjoy yourself complements of your county commissioners." Then there they are listed all over again. I've seen the three of them how many times so far today? You jest can't escape these guys and their free advertisin. At least there's no meters in the parkin lot here so I pull the Jimmy into one of the spaces. I can't help fumin about those guys tryin to take all the credit for the park. This place wuz donated to the county by the Warner family years ago. Samuel J. Warner wuz a salesman for the iron works back in the good old days. His family wuz one of the original settlers of Possum Crossing and they accumulated quite a bit of land in and around town. Werner Warner wuz the grandfather of Samuel who loved the idea of a park in Possum. Matter of fact Werner tried his darndest to git the city fathers to build a zoo. Werner wanted to bring in lions, tigers, leopards, bears, etc., and have them housed right here in town. No elephants, hippos, buffaloes or any of that sort. Jest animals to fit in the cages to be built in the hollow of the park. A mini zoo you might call it. Well, after some negotiatin, folks thought it might make Possum a real tourist attraction. The bear's den and caged areas for the cats were soon constructed. Original plans went awry when they determined that the cost of obtainin such critters would exceed the town treasury.

So when Samuel became the top salesman for the iron works he revived the idea of the park. It would be minus the animals Werner had wanted but would be a nice attraction for the town. So it came into bein jest like it is today. The family donated the land and the park consisted of a play area for the small kids, a baseball field, an area for picnics and such and the hollow with the still unfinished zoo. The commissioners did furnish the kids area with swings and slides and other gizmos what keeps kids busy and out of trouble. The baseball field wuz laid out and bleachers were constructed for spectators. It got a lot of use years ago when kids would take a ball and bat and form up teams. Today kids is busy playin games on their Iphones and Xboxes. It mostly gits used by families durin their picnics. There is also a quiet, shady part with picnic tables laid out under some great oaks and maple trees. They provide plenty of shade for picnickers.

I head for the quiet, shady area with the intention of enjoyin my burger and fries. There's a table with no one else in sight so I set down and open up my lunch. No sooner had I taken a couple of bites of the burger than I hears a voice: "Hey, Cliff Paulsen, looks like we got the same lunch today" he says while holdin up a Wendy's bag a wavin it back and forth. He looks at me and says "lettuce, tomato & mayo I'll bet."

I shake my head and say "mustard, pickle & onion. I would have given you three guesses but figgered it would take too long."

"Ha, ha, ha. That's a good one. Yep, that's a good one. Mind if I sit here?" He says as he plops down almost directly across from me.

"Go on and take a seat, Snuffy" I says reluctantly.

Snuffy Smith lives in an old house down by the river. Closer to the river than most folks would be willin to live. Snuffy, I honestly can't remember his real first name but I believe it to be Alexander Aloysius, used to live in Mrs. Millbourne's boardin house. Wuz one of long time boarders as I recall. One day Snuffy decided he wanted to buy a home of his own. As luck would have it Mrs. Trafford who had lived down by the river wuz lookin to sell her place.

Now you got to understand the Trafford place. The Traffords wuz one of the early Possum families. Can't say exactly when they arrived in town but it wuz early on when Possum wuz still puttin on her baby fat. Anyhow, they settled on land down near the river on Possum Point. It wuz dern near the river where they placed their home. The house wuz constructed on high ground on the point and had one of most beautifulest views of the river in Possum. They could see way up and down the river in either direction. There wuz quite a view of the evenin sunset and their access to the river wuz the envy of all in town. Quentin Trafford installed a boat dock and put up the barn aways back from the rivers edge. The land all about wuz farmed all through the early years. Quentin even constructed a stone wall about four feet tall to protect the house from floodin when the Ohio went on one of its rampages. He wuz quite the engineer as it seems since Ohio flood waters usually stayed behind the wall. Through the years though the river traffic grew and them tugs and barges got bigger and bigger. They dredged the river and put in dams to maintain an acceptable water level. That wuz real great for river traffic but the flood waters came up a bit higher and the Ohio seemed to take out her fury on all these intruders. Well it didn't give the Traffords no never mind. They jest accepted the perils for the right to put down here on the nicest spot in the area.

The place changed over the years with an addition here and somethin subtacted there but durin all this time it remained as the Trafford home. Ellie and Melvin were the last Traffords to occupy the house and farm. The family grew smaller thru the years as traffic accidents, illness, losses in the war and suicides took a mighty big toll. Ellie wuz the last one left after Melvin done shot hisself in the barn one day. He wuz missin for a couple a days afore neighbors helpin to look for him found the body. Ellie continued to stay in the home even after the funeral and burial. She no longer operated it as a farm though. The livestock wuz all sold off and the fields were left to return to their better nature.

Floods threatened the widow many times but the wall did its job as Quentin had intended. On a couple of occasions water spilled over the wall. In the past Melvin had always been there to sandbag when the waters threatened but with him gone Ellie wuz left to fend for herself. This last flood five years ago wuz the flood that broke the Trafford's back. Water came up over the wall and right up to the house door. After payin its "howdy do, Mrs. Ellie, I'm here to visit with ya fer a spell," it entered the door. "You won't mind if I jest come inside and make myself at home." That's jest what the river did. It went inside and took possession of the entire first floor leavin Ellie to scramble to the upper floor. She wuz stranded there until the Possum Volunteer Fire Department crew rowed up to a second floor window and pulled the widow to safety. There wuz cheers and applause all around as the boat docked and the widow wuz lifted safely to the shore.

When the waters finally receded Ellie went back to take a look at the place. The river left its gifts to thank Ellie for the hospitality as it went back to its regular course. Mud, debris of all sorts littered the house and farmyard. Ellie cried and asked to be taken to the Crestview Acres Retirement Home back up on Crestview heights. There she remained while figgerin out what her future would be.

It wuz tough for her to come to a decision to sell so she pondered for over two years afore makin her choice. It would be Crestview and the farm would be up for sale. Now this wuz not the ideal time to be asellin real estate in Possum. Most folks were in no position to buy and the banks were of the same mind. The Real Estate Transactions section of the Times wuz usually bare as ole Mother Hubbard's. The house wuz a wreck and the barn wuz practically fallin down from misuse and neglect. There wuz ads for the place left with no responses and the price kept droppin in the hope of attractin a bite. Most folks didn't like the idea of all that cleanup.

Snuffy Smith ain't most folks though. He went through the place and saw all the mud caked dry on the floor and walls, debris still scatterd about and the MOLD. Black mold wuz everywhere and would take quite a cleanin to remove it. Snuffy had enough of livin as a boarder at Mrs. Millbournes. Mrs. Edwina Millbournes had been takin in boarders ever since her husband Fred keeled over at the supper table right into his plate of ham hocks and beans. Three squares and a bed is what them boarders got. They all shared one bath and the linens wuz changed weekly. There wuz always bacon and eggs for breakfast; a lunch bag wuz provided with a sandwich of some sort of lunchmeat and cookie; and dinner wuz served promptly at five o'clock on the dot. If you weren't seated at the table with your napkin tucked neatly under your chin you would have to go elsewhere for your supper. No esplanations, no excuses. If you weren't seated you didn't eat.

I think the last straw wuz the stew she served up one evening. The men sat around the table as usual. It wuz five o'clock sharp and napkins were tucked and hands were armed with their utensils as the men awaited the arrival of "Grandma Millbournes' mouth waterin beef stew." Mrs. Millbournes set down the tureen of home made beef stew as the hard workin crew wuz ready to dig in. Artie Finebush did the honors of servin up the stew. He grabbed the ladle and started fillin up the bowls.

"What the ****. What is that?" someone blurted out as Finebush lifted the ladle high. It looked like a large rat hangin and about to drop back into the stewpot. Afore anyone could say a futher word, Mrs. Millbournes wuz on scene grabbin the object while it wuz still bein held high and closely examined. She quickly grabbed hold of the thing and wuz carryin it through the dinin room while the stew broth wuz drippin down to the floor.

"That there's jest the grease rag from greasin the top of the bread loaves. I adds that to provide a little extry flavor to the stew." She exited the room and had little more to say.

Snuffy says to the fella sittin next to him, "looks a lot like the rags she wraps around her legs to help her arthuritis to me."

The rag and the hunks of floatin beef fat turned off all but the truly starving. Twernt long after that Snuffy set about lookin for another place.

The Trafford place wuz jest what he wuz lookin for and the price wuz well within his reach. Yep, it was within his reach after he did a mighty fine bit a negotiatin. He done got Ellie to sign over the place for $500.00. Told her he wuz goin to fix it up so's it would look like it always did. He might even bring back the cattle and horses after the barn wuz repaired. She could come visit and set down by the river any time she pleased. That last part wuz enough to make her sign on the dotted line. Settin by the river and watchin the tows go by jest like she and Melvin had done so many times in the past.

Well, Snuffy got the debris removed and a lot of stuff burned in a huge bonfire. He tried to do a little repairin on the barn but his pals convinced him that the roof wuz too far gone and about to cave in. So he stopped workin on the barn and went back to gittin the house tidied up a bit. Ole Snuffy wuz on the disability on account of his bad back. That there disability wuz sure a blessin to Snuffy because without it he could have never gotten rid of the black mold. "That there mold is a health hazard," they told him and offered to take care of it. They brought in some big time outfit from Pittsburgh (or "Picksburg" as Snuffy likes to say) and they went over the house from top to bottom. He claims the cost wuz ten times what he paid for the house. Never worried him a bit. The disability folks took care of the entire bill and installed a new roof to boot.

I jest about choked on my last bite of the burger when Snuffy started rattlin off the numbers of the benefits he got. A $500.00 house gits the gov ment treatment thanks to disability; a $5000.00 mold abatement; a $4800.00 roof. They dumped twenty times his purchase price into a house of questionable viability. Now if I wuz stupid enough to buy a house what done been through the flood and is crawlin with black mold I would expect to take my chances and live in it or git to work cleanin it like my life depended on it. Not these folks today. No matter what kind of mess they done gits into the gov ment is goin to come along and make it all the better no matter what the cost. Jest like your mama when you wuz a baby. No wonder Snuffy is settin there grinnin like a pig what done broke its way into the feed barn. I am stuffin in the last French fry and thinkin to myself how these French fries are good but can't compare with the French fries made by Mrs. James at Five Mile Point. My Ma used to say "There's no French fries like Mrs. James' fries." Yep, she sure was right. It wuz like eatin candy to a young lad of five years of age. Now I'm debatin whether I really want to finish off that extra large drink when Sue Ann Barkley approaches our table.

"Afternoon, gentlemen. I wuz wonderin if you'd be interested in signin our petition," she says.

I ain't seen Sue Ann in month of sunny days as the sayin goes. What the heck could she be askin for now? Sue Ann ain't shy so she plunks the papers down right on the table between us. Snuffy looks at me with the same puzzled look as I.

"We are petitionin the county commissioners so that they will reconsider their vote to cancel the contract with the animal shelter association."

She don't have to do any more esplainin to me since I've been readin all about this here fracas in the Times. Now the shelter association has been runnin the county animal shelter for quite a few years. They take in lost and stray cats and dogs and provides their eats, shots, neuterin and sleepin quarters. They try to find new homes that wish to adopt these helpless critters. Some folks refer to them as a "no kill" shelter. I think there are times when a critter is so sick or injured that they has no choice but to put it out of its misery. It's done humanely of course. Most residents of McCorkle County approves their work overwhelmingly. Matter of fact last fall we had the animal shelter levy on the ballot and it got a 78% approval vote. That there gives them three commissioners the power to place a tax on every homeowner in the county. It raises a significant amount of the associations budget. They gits some other $$$ through donations and the like.

Now commissioners bein the sneaky types that they are made sure the voters approved the levy first. The money is now in their grubby hands. Months later they tell the association that it is time to put the shelter operation out for bids. There ain't but one bidder wishin to take on this burden—the animal shelter association. Are you ready for the tricksters to pull their trick? OK. The commissioners say to the association "now if you jest sign this contract we can have you begin operations in the new fiscal year". Knowin full well who they are dealin with, the association decides to go over this contract with a rooster's comb as the sayin goes. Article 3, section 8, paragraph 5 clearly states that the operator of the shelter will comply with state law that requires euthanasia for any animal in the shelter for more than five days. This is contrary to how the shelter has been operated for the last dozen years. They try to negotiate but the three stone hearts have nothin to say and as a matter of fact refuse to even answer voters questions when they take the time to show up at commission meetings. The three stone faces sit there starin at the audience while keepin entirely silent. By the time the deadline has arrived for awardin the contract the stone heads announce that since no one has accepted the contract the county must run the shelter itself. Guess who gits to keep the levy money for its own use? Guess who is willin and ready to obey the five day euthanizin clause?

Snuffy and myself gladly add our John Henrys to the long list of petitioners. Sue Ann departs to solicit other signatures for her petition. "Poor girl" I say to Snuffy.

"Yeah I know them dern dunderheads at the courthouse ain't goin to pay no heed to that there petition. They has done got their way and that's that," he replies.

Snuffy has a couple tears flowin down his cheeks. This is about the limit of my ability to tolerate this here nonsense so I says "excuse me Snuffy but I gotta run now. Lots of errands for the wife ya know."

Snuffy stays settin there and waves his hand to say good bye.

## Chapter VIII A Possum Goes Shoppin

I gits back to the Jimmy and wish I didn't have to make the trip down to New Hickory. It's not that I mind the drivin but the thought of goin to Wal Mart at this time of month is almost more than a poor soul can bear. The first of the month is when all them checks come in and them cards git refilled so it will be packed in every department. I done promised the wife I would pick up one of them oscillatin floor fans and I better git one afore they is all gone.

As I'm drivin on my way I spot Chester Dayrimple hitchin along side the road. I pulls the Jimmy to the side of the road and lowers the window. "Hey, Chester, you be aheadin to Newie?" Any idiot can figger that a man standin along side this road hitchin could only be headin one way.

I guess it must be force of habit sort of like askin a man with a fishin pole in hand if he is goin fishin. Anyhow, Chester's got a broad grin like he done hit the lotto and reaches for the door handle. "Man, Cliff, do I appreciate the ride. That sun's gittin hot enough to fry ham and eggs on the roadway."

Now you got to know Chester to expect that kinda talk. Chester only made it through sixth grade in school. He's about the only kid who hated school more than I did. One day he actually jumped out the school window while Miss Inch wasn't lookin. Took off for the rest of the afternoon and nobody caught him. I may be stretchin it a bit when I say he made it through sixth grade. Actually, Chester flunked 6th grade three times. The principal and Miss Inch finally determined that there weren't no use goin through this process since there wuz absolutely no hope Chester wuz goin to do any better in school. Sides, he wuz gittin a good bit bigger and older than the other kids in class. It wuz tough fittin him in those desks designed for smaller kids. So they jest passed him on from year to year until he wuz finally able to drop out all together.

"Yeah, I'm headin over to Wal Mart to pick up a fan for the wife. House has been pretty hot here lately."

"It's that global warmin climate change" Chester replies. "I hears on the TV that we is gittin so hot that the polar ice is meltin and the earth is goin to git flooded when the ocean fills up."

"Now, Chester, "I say "you know the ocean is full as it's goin to git and that's jest some scare tactics to git everybody riled up."

"Oh no, this ain't no scare stuff. We is makin so much pollution that the atmosphere is warmin and the planets is gittin hotter than ever."

"Planets," I blurt out. "What do you mean planets?"

"Like I seen on the TV. They say Mars and Jupiter is warmin up too."

"How can that be?" I question.

"It's all these cars and coal burnin lectric plants that is puttin out too much pollution. That there pollution rises up to the sky and collects in the atmosphere of the planets."

"How does that make Mars and Jupiter warmer?"

"Pollution rises and is carried on the wind for as far as the eye can see, night or day. I know it for a fact. I seen it on the weather channel. We is in big trouble."

I know this conversation is goin nowheres so I decide to change the subject. "Whatcha been up to lately?"

"Oh, I been workin on my bike. Matter of fact that's why I need to go to Newie. I needs to git a new "tar" for it. I done patched the old one up so many times it jest won't hold air any more. They got a special deal at Wal Mart so I might even take a look at a new bike. I doubt that I can afford a new one, though, Mom says I got to save my money for the old age like she is. You know the sayin 'a penny earned is a penny saved.'"

"You're right on that one, we got to save our pennies in times like these."

"Mrs. Barkhouse saves her pennies for me. I got quite a collection of them. Usually I looks around the bank parkin lot for change people drops. There's good ones there and over at Frankies. I figger this here bag must have a few dollars worth by now," he says as he holds up an old brown paper bag about as fat as a large grapefruit. He shakes the bag a few times to let me know it is full.

"You goin to buy a tar with that, are ya?" I say as he shakes the bag some more.

"Oh, yeah, I may even have enough for that new bike. I'm goin to put these pennies in the machine and git dollars for them."

"Why didn't you jest count them afore you left?" I ask stupidly. I say stupidly because the question causes him to laugh uncontrollably.

"It don't make no sense countin your money when they have machines at Wal Mart what does it for ya. Mom says wasted labor is the devil's workshop. I ain't about to start workin for no devil, I don't even work for the man."

Now that lad ain't had much schoolin but he's sure right about workin. He seen plenty of folks in Possum who found out how much easier it is to not work when you have the choice. Time wuz when you didn't work you didn't eat. Now you eats real good when you don't work.

We gits to Wal Mart and sure enough the parkin lot is near full. It means we will have to course up and down the aisles till we find a suitable spot. Suitable cause there is plenty of spaces remainin for "handicapped only" and "expectant mothers" and "mothers with small babies" and probably some for "persons learnin to drive." It ticks me when I see folks with these here "handicapped" signs hangin from their mirrors git out and walk gingerly to the door. It must be that I'm handicapped too. Dern it. That blue Dodge beat me to that spot. If only I hadn't been held up waitin in line for them that's waitin for a body to pull out. I hates comin here on the first of the month.

Finally we reach the aisle all the way down by the garden center. There's some vacant spots available so I makes my move. Ha, ha, beat that red Jeep to the space. "Well, Chester, I guess I'll be a seein ya," I say as I'm openin my door to the blazin hot air of the parkin lot.

"Say, if you don't mind I'd like to tag along with ya. I might want to git Mom one of them there fans too. Sides, I'll be needin a ride back to Possum if you have it in your heart to give one."

Now if that don't beat all. I gives a man a ride to Newie and he asks if he can have a ride back to Possum. Like I'm runnin a cab service or somethin. He's standin there holdin that bag of pennies and lookin at me like I ain't got no heart if I don't let him ride back with me. "Come on," I say, "but you better not hold me up lookin at them bikes. I got to git back to Possum with the fan or I'll git an ass chewin from little miss pretty one."

We go inside and find most of the carts are gone. There's quite a few out in the parkin area in them corrals but I'm not up to walkin back out in that heat. We jest waits there for a time and sure enough a mess more gits shoved through the cart doors. "Could ya wait jest a second while I runs these pennies through the machine?" Oh, yeah, I got plenty of time to spare and what's another second or two? I think to myself.

"Go on git your money. I'll wait fer ya." Now when you dump your coins into that machine it takes more than a second to count them out and figger your total. I said I would wait and I'm usually a man of my word.

Whilest I'm waitin I study all these folks pokin at all the fruits and veggies. Most don't intend to buy them anyways, they jest likes pokin around. Usually they will fill their carts with the ready-made stuff since that'd be a lot easier to microwave. Dern if I don't observe the fat of the earth. I don't skimp on eatin, myself, but these folks ain't never missed a meal or a snack. I see legs that look like the old stump of the maple tree which used to grace the front of my yard. Sure enough the go-cart people are here. Oxygen tubes plugged in their noses and fat overhangin the cart. There's barely enough room when two of them want to pass each other. Sometimes I think they wanted to be Nascar drivers but as life would have it they are confined to racin around the aisles of the Wal Mart. There is almost a collision between a senior citizen and a woman who can barely maneuver through the aisles. That wuz close to be sure.

A woman dressed in a halter top and short shorts comes through the door. She has three kids in tow and one of them pushes her cart right into mine. "Taylor, watch where you're goin or I'm goin to let Jeffie push the cart," she says without so much as an "I'm sorry" to me. Think nothin of it lady, I like gittin smashed by shoppin carts, a few bruises to the gluteous maximus makes a man more attractive I think to myself. Where's that Chester? That second has gone on for several minutes now. Jest about then I spot him walkin back toward me.

"What took you so long?"

"Oh, sorry bout that. There wuz a line and I had to wait. Got my money though."

"Come on. Let's git goin so we can git outta here."

I'm pushin my empty cart back to git the fan while Chester keeps fingerin his money. "You better put that in your pocket afore some of those bills go flyin down the aisle," I caution him.

We reach the display of fans and air conditioners after inchin our way through the congestion of carts. Gall, dern. The oscillatin floor fans is all gone! Now I'm in deep doodoo. How do I esplain that I missed out on the fans cause I wuz waitin for Chester Dayrimple to count his pennies?

Jest about that time a Wal Mart Associate comes pushin a dolly loaded with fans. I didn't wait for him to unload the merchandise. I grabbed the model my wife wanted and plopped it down into my cart. "Jest what I've been lookin for" I blurt out to the astonished associate. "Let's go, Chester, you've got five minutes to look at those bikes," I say as we dash down the aisle.

When we git to the bicycles, Chester's eyes git big as the moon when it comes up over Snyder's Hill. "Look at them bikes, wouldja. They got so many to choose from. This here's a nice one. Oh, look at that. Reflectors, lights and all. What color do you think would be a good pick? How about that purple one? That would be the envy of everyone in Possum. Bet people would want me to lead the Fourth of July parade with that one."

"Chester," I finally say, "how much money have you got in your pocket?" He reaches inside and pulls out the wad of cash and begins countin. After goin through the wad of cash a few times he blurts out "sixteen dollars."

"Sixteen dollars?"

"Yep, I'm afraid I lied to you about my bag bein pennies. There wuz quarters and dimes and a few nickles. I found them all on the ground around town and Mom says if you sees it lyin around that is like money from heaven. That's what they say in the movies 'Pennies from Heaven'. You won't say nothin to nobody will ya?"

"Nah, I'm not goin to snitch on ya but why are you lookin at these bikes? That sixteen dollars is not enough for any of them. Why would you want them anyway? I'll bet they re all made in China. Look at that metal. It's not the quality of your bike. Yours is American made and good and solid. It puts these here things to shame. These aren't even worth carryin back home to Possum."

"Ah, guess you're right. These things can't hold a candle to my Gertie. That's what I call her, Gertie. She's still betterin than any of these."

"Let's go pick up the 'tar'. You got enough cash for that and sides that tar will make her good as new."

So we are done with the shoppin but can we go home? OK, not quite so fast you Wal Mart shoppers. There it is; thirty-two ultra modern check out lines jest waitin with open arms. Open arms? Well not today my dear fine friend. Today is the day of the Invader! And here they are like the plains buffaloes of long ago. Millin and maneuverin into pens so that their goods may be run through that electronic marvel: the check out scanner. I admit that I have no knowledge of how the dern thing works. Some how when the associate runs your item over this glass window in the counter the name of the item and the price shows up on the screen. They say there's a device under that glass which looks at them little lines on your item and can figger out what the item is and what the price is also. Now that there is enough to make your head spin that a device which you can't even see has the smarts to do all that. But as they say on TV "wait there's more." That there mystery device also adds up the price of your items and prints out a tape listin all them items along with the price for you to take with you.

Over in Possum, we hain't got a single one of these electronic devices but here in Wal Mart they have thirty-two of the gall dern things. I don't know if this is progress or what. It seems to me that the gov ment could place some of these marks on your arm or hand and they would know everythin about you. Let's see, they could tell your age, sex, color of eyes, hair (only sometimes in the case of females), illnesses, where you went to school. How about your blood type, what vaccines you had and even if you smoke, drink or have some rare disease. Why there ain't no end to what that device could tell them. It's even scarier since they don't have to slide you down a counter cause they can hold one of them devices in their hand and zap, it has the same info. I knowed the first time I saw one that they wuz a might scary. Preacher Wainwright says they might become the "mark of the beast."

I'm standin there thinkin these profound thoughts when I am distracted by the forward movement of my line. Three people still ahead of me! You think that because you are in a line with only three persons ahead of you at register #17 that you will have a short wait time. You want to put a gold star on your forehead for this gem of a thought. Ordinarily good thinkin but not on Wal Mart Invader Days. Take a closer look at that line. Each of them three people have at least two full carts. I say at least because one has three carts and they is bein minded by the toddlers. First there are three and then there are seven in front of you. What can you do? Panic and go look for a shorter line? No, no, my friend; you would lose your place in line to somewheres with only miniscule odds of findin a better place.

So here you stay watchin the kids climb all over the carts and the little one tucked in the cart seat grabbin for all the candies and gum in sight. "No, Dakota," mom says as she takes the goodies from the child's hand and places it back on the display. "Quit climbin on the cart," she says to another. "You're goin to git yer ass whipped fer sher when we git home." She's tryin to place items on the counter and control her brood at the same time. Bein that she's got but two hands and two eyes this is a formidable task, and she's pregnant to boot.

The line jest keeps inchin forward and you keep lookin hopin to see a break in the traffic open up. They have carts overflowin with goods and here I stand with a cart containin a floor fan and a bicycle tar. Ordinarily, there would be registers open with service for persons with less than twenty items. There is such a crush of shoppers today that the lights on all of them are dark. Finally I git to the point where I am about to pick up my fan and place it on the conveyor belt.

"No need to take that out, sir. I can come around and git it." At last I am gittin a break on this trip. She leaves her post and comes around to my side of the conveyor. In her hand is one of those hand held price zappers. You know that dern thing that Preacher Wainwright says is part of that "mark of the beast program" the gov ment is goin to spring on us one of these days. The zapper does its thing and she says "that'll be $74.83 please."

"Hold on there jest a minute. That fan is on sale for $59.87. That's quite a bit of tax, isn't it?" She looks down at the tape and then at the sale tag and frowns a bit. "I'll have to call a supervisor. Jest a moment."

With that she sets her light flashin and everyone is standin with hands on their hips. I can feel the ugliness beginnin to build in the people in line behind me. Even I begin to adopt a rather impatient mood. The supervisor finally arrives and she looks at the fan; then looks at the tape; then looks at the flyer. Finally she is satisfied that I am not fakin the whole thing and takes her keys and unlocks the register. She fiddles around with the thing then nods to the cashier. Oh boy. She cancels the former sale and repeats the whole process again. This time she rings up the correct price and I am ready to depart. "I'm very sorry about that, sir." I start to push forward toward the door when I remember Chester still has to git through the gall dern thing with his bike tar so I pause midway and wait.

At last we head back to our parkin space with our goodies. Some idiot hasn't bothered to return their cart to the cart corral and it has drifted downhill, pickin up speed as it went, only to crash into another shopper's car. Too bad you can't catch these lazy s.o.b.'s and have fifty other shoppers propel their carts downhill at his car. By now you must have figgered out that this parkin lot is not flat but is one with a pretty decent grade to it. If you drop a can of beans or a basketball you can bet they will reach bottom at such a speed as you could never hope to stop them.

## Chapter IX  Storm A Brewin

Out we go to git into the line headin out of the lot and back onto the highway. We have only gone down the road a piece when Chester spots the sign for an ice cream place with 32 flavors. "Do you suppose we could stop and git a cone?" he asks. Feelin that this may be a good chance to git some relief from Chester's incessant jabberin about Gertie and how she's goin to be thrilled with her new "tar", I figger it might be a good idea.

We go inside and I can already feel the beneficial effects of the extra cool shop. Sure enough, they have every flavor you could imagine. We both study the selections carefully causin you don't git an opportunity like this everyday. I expect Chester will go for peanut butter 'n' jelly and chocolate and marshmallows or some such other weird concoction.

"I'd like somethin hot on a day like this. I'll have a hot fudge sundae. Mama says you should eat warm things on a hot day and cool things on a cold day. It equalizes the body temperature," he esplains. He's orderin ice cream for Pete's sake and vanilla to boot. Thirty-two flavors and he picks somethin we could git back in Possum! What do I know? I ain't no Baskin or Robbins.

We sit down at a small table and begin to enjoy our treats when a familiar face from Possum, Tom McFarlan, appears outta nowhere. "Hi, guys. Imagine meetin you here."

I manage a curt "Yeah" but Chester starts blabbin how we went to Wal Mart; what we got; what happened while there and how we are headed back to Possum now. Can you beat that? We're on the road which leads to only one place and Chester has to esplain that.

"Say would you fellas happen to have a little space for a nuther headin back to Possum woudja?" Tom asks.

Oh great, first there wuz one and now there are two. "Sure. We got plenty of room in the truck and you can put those bags in the back."

Well now old Tom starts tearin up like a new born. "Thank you, thank you. You are so kind to unburden me from the long walk back to Possum. I got this here stuff for my Ma. You know she's been in a wheelchair ever since her bout with cancer and losin poor Pa in that car crash. She still loves to knit even though they say she's got the Old Timer's disease. It's her only pleasure left in life and she jest loves all these purdy colors they have at Wal Marts."

I'm thinkin, OK, Tom, knock it off you got your ride back to Possum and I suppose you want me to take you all the way up Roosevelt Drive and drop you off at your front door.

That's one thing I forgot to tell y'all when I wuz describin the town. The streets is all named for presidents of the USA. The major ones got named Washington, Lincoln, Grant, Jefferson, Adams, etc. and the lessor ones got Polk, Taylor, Hayes, McKinley and so on. The cross streets is all named First, Second, Third, etc. It's a pretty important thing in town to live at the ideal spots. You know, First and Washington; Sixteenth and Lincoln; Third and Jefferson and so forth. I'm not one of the lucky ones myself. I live on Lincoln Street but not anywheres near Sixteenth.

Gettin back to Tom, who is still standin alongside our table, I say "well, Tom, you can jest drop them bags in the back of the Jimmy and hop inside with us. We're about ready to head on out now."

"Wait jest a second" he replies. My elbow rests on the table as my hand and forehead meet. Seems I've already heard that phrase not too long ago and I remember what happened then.

"I don't wish to be the bearer of bad news or nuthin but I checked my IPhone and a terrific storm is goin to hit tween here and Possum any minute now."

"You did what?" I ask in a rather loud voice.

"See, look here at my IPhone. I tap the 'Storm' app and git the rain and lightnin reports for our area. Look at that red and orange and all those lightnin bolts."

"Tom," I say, "that is jest a weather forecast and I don't see how that IPhone of yours could know our weather now."

"No, no, no. This is no ordinary forecast. This here's actual reports of lightnin strikes and a radar image of what's ahead. See this 'ALERT' for severe thunderstorm headin right towards us. It's projected to hit in seven minutes. Possum is already takin a poundin from the dern thing."

While takin the last bite of my cone, I glance out the window and spy a really dark sky which is dark enough to git the lights goin on. Perhaps Tom is onto somethin after all. "How did you say you got that on your IPhone?" I inquire.

"I used this here 'Storm' app. See you jest push here and look at them lightnin bolts everywhere." I peer at the infernal gadget and observe bolts of lightnin everywhere. Too many for me to count.

"OK!" I say, "you've convinced me" jest as heavy rain begins to pelt the windows and the trees start swayin in the wind.

KABOOM! There wuz a flash of lightnin and a blast what done rattled the windows of the place. The whole placed jumped with fright and the clerk knocked a milk shake all over the counter. A few people with napkins in hand go to her aid. But then, KABOOM AND KABOOM, more lightnin. The wind is blowin so hard you can barely see through the rain which is now lashin at the windows like some mighty giant with a fire hose. Some flyin debris bangs against the windows and a lot of folks hit the floor. Chester, Tom and myself duck behind the counter figgerin we will have some protection in case of flyin glass. The way those windows are rattlin there's no tellin how long they is goin to hold.

I lose count of the KABOOMS as I'm concentratin on holdin on to somethin solid in case the place blows away. The lights begin to flicker and then they all go dark. Chester says "do you think we should pray? Mama says when there is a bad storm you should pray." "That sure sounds like a good idea to me and right now I can't think of anythin "....KABOOM, followed by an even closer KABOOM. You can hear the ice pellets bouncin off the windows and I is beginnin to worry about how much more they can take. Then there seems to be a miracle from heaven.

Slowly the storm seems to be lessenin. The wind is not drivin directly against the windows now and you can see it is a bit brighter outside. I go closer so I can git a better view. The ground is white jest like after a snow shower. It ain't snow though; it's hail. It looks to be a half-inch deep all over the parkin lot. I look over at my truck to see if I still have a windshield. All the vehicles in the lot look to be OK cept for the hail and other debris on them. Oops, a light pole at the end of the lot has snapped and come down. Luckily nobody had parked close to the light. It may have been the cause of our power loss. You can still hear thunder in the distance and now there are sirens screamin all over town. A "far" truck comes racin by with red lights flashin and sirens goin full blast. Folks are shakin all over inside the ice cream shop. I ask the clerk if she needs any help but she shakes her head to indicate 'no'. We wait a while and the rain has stopped completely. It seems to be safe enough to go outside and begin clearin the hail pellets off my truck. Chester and Tom lend a hand gittin it cleared. It looks like it may have taken a few dings but it's hard to tell for sure. I'll check it out more thoroughly onest we git back to Possum.

I look at Chester and Tom and say "well, what do you think? Should we try to git back to Possum now?"

They glance at each other and Tom is first to speak "Why not? There ain't no use remainin here. Let's git on the road and see what it's like."

With that we climb into the Jimmy and head out of the parkin lot. We only git as far as the intersection with the highway when we encounter a cop directin traffic. He points to us and then in the direction of Possum. I take a quick glance to my left and spot lots of flashin red lights. It looks like the main part of the storm went toward New Hickory proper. There's a lot of leafs and small branches scattered all over the road in addition to hail settin alongside our lane. "We sure wuz lucky, boys. I would hate to see what that storm done did to Newie" I say.

Chester responds "what about Possum? Do you suppose it did much damage there?" "Well, we is goin to find out pretty soon. It shouldn't be long afore we can check it out."

We git a few miles down the road when I see more flashin red lights. A state trooper's car is in our lane and a state highway truck is jest ahead of him. A rather large tree has come down and is partially blockin the highway. The trooper motions for us to move to the other lane and move on. Ahead is an ambulance with lights flashin and paramedics attendin to someone. There is a pile up of three cars which look like they has hit head on. Glass and metal is scattered about and some fluid is poolin on the blacktop.

"Wow, take a look at that! They must have been blinded by the rain," Tom says in a panicky voice.

"Yeah," Chester responds, "good thing we stopped for that ice cream."

"You're right, Chester, this wuz one time when you gave us a good tip," I respond gratefully.

Tom speaks up "and what about me? What if I had been awalkin on this road? I might have been blown clean into the river."

"We all can thank our guardin angels for savin us this time," I respond.

The rest of the trip is uneventful. We detour around a few branches across the highway and arrive back at Possum. It doesn't appear that there is too much damage as far as I can see. Oh, there is branches down and trash cans rollin along the main street. We can see a few flashin lights along the side streets and the power seems to be out since traffic lights are not workin. Nothin is causin us any trouble as we make our way to Roosevelt Drive. At last we arrive at Tom's house which looks like it didn't suffer any damage. Tom thanks me profusely and grabs his bags from the back of the truck. We wave goodbye and head for Chester's place. No damage apparent there so he departs and I head back home.

It don't take me long to realize that Possum is not so lucky as I had thought. Now I live at 341 West Lincoln Street which is several blocks from Taylor Street where I dropped Chester off. First I catches sight of flashin red and blue lights directly ahead of me. Then a cop in the intersection, cause the traffic lights is not workin, motions to me to make a detour from my intended route.

I can easily see plenty of downed trees and lectric lines in the street. Each street I pass seems to have the same problem; it's impassable. Finally after goin about four blocks out of my way I come to Harrison street which appears to have no emergency vehicles on it. One thing for sure, I won't have to worry about downed trees here cause they ain't got any trees growed on that street. You can see plenty of debris; papers, boxes, kids bicycles and the like, strewn all around. It causes me no problem dodgin the stuff and I'm able to git by without hittin any of this gall dern modern day litter.

West Harrison ain't one of the better streets in town and neither is East Harrison for that matter. Folks livin on this street is commonly known as "hoopies." You know, like them hot shots from Wheeling who used to make hoops for barrels back in the olden times. They's all characters livin here mostly takin whatever Uncle offers them if you know what I mean. Take that double wide there at 572, that's the Schuler residence; Jethro and Heather Jane Schuler that is to say. They really ain't married in the usual way. Jethro is nineteen and Heather is but eighteen years of age. They done already had three kids and Heather is expectin again. Jethro don't work on account of he's got a "bad back" and of course he's got the disability check a comin in every month. They qualify for the WIC and the CHIP and the kids got daycare provided. They gits that cause Heather "works" part time down at the Women's Health Services. She don't work enough to git enough pay to live on so she is eligible for benefits. Jim Baxter told me that Jethro does a little moonlightin over at Peterson Auto Repair and gas station. He ain't on the "books" though since he is paid under the table in cash. They didn't buy that double wide either since Heather's Pa done got the title. That means the young couple don't have no assets which would interfere with their benefits. Jethro drives an old Ford truck which is also "owned" by Heather's Pa.

Some folks say Jethro also picks up a little spendin money sellin some Mary Jane on the side. We gots a real problem here in town lately with these young folk smokin dope. That ain't all either. The Times has had reports of the heroin comin into town from some big city dealers. There has been a number of cases at the hospital of folks brought in after over-dosin on the stuff. Laurie Ann Baker, a nurse at the local hospital, told me that onest she gave a double dose of the Narcan, which is a antidote, to an overdose victim who wuz brought into the emergency room. Accordin to Laurie Ann the woman wuz near death. She done woke up after gittin the antidote and started cussin out poor Laurie Ann for "ruinin her high". She even threatenin to give Laurie Ann a "sock in the face" for interferin with her. Laurie Ann don't take no guff from these characters so she says "go ahead and try it. There's a cop standin right outside that door." Didn't hear another peep from that dopehead.

You can't never tell what you is goin to encounter when dealin with these dope heads. The sheriff, "Mr. Mustache", we likes to call him since he sports one of them gall dern fancy hair things under his nose, keeps tellin everybody how he's got this thing under investigation. He may be investigatin but he's not done much to stop it. Folks is gittin pretty fed up with all the petty thefts which is goin on around town. Those disability payments jest don't go far enough when you got a habit like the heroin. Did I tell ya how much I hates mustaches?

I jest passed the Finklestine Apartments. That there is what you call the "low income" housing project. If you don't make enough or you are on some sort of welfare you qualify for reduced rental payments. It's a nice arrangement if you don't mind bein on the dole. Take Sally Sue Hainesworth for example. That girl has six kids which belong to four different daddies. She gits the basic unit for a much lower price than you would expect. She is only responsible for twenty dollars on her electric bill. Seein that them there places is all electric that is a dern good deal. Wish I could git my electric bill for twenty dollars! Every month the gall dern thing is a goin up and up. If the price gits any higher I'll jest have to go off the grid.

Speakin of off the grid, lots of folks is turnin to them there wood burnin stoves for heatin nowadays. I'd be willin to bet Jethro Schuler is somewhere over on them streets cuttin up fallen trees with Heather's "daddy's chain saw." He'll haul them back over here and use her "daddy's log splitter" to make "far" wood. Gits a good price for a cord, all in cash, of course.

I'm turnin on to Third Street and can jest about see my house on West Lincoln. Can't see much damage here ceptin a few tree limbs in the street and no lectric power. It's goin to be good to git back home after a day like this. The wife should be pretty happy with her new oscillatin floor fan. She won't believe the trouble I has gone to jest to git this gadget for her. You don't suppose she'll be disappointed that she won't be able to try it out jest now. Ah, heck, with all this trouble today a little wait for the power to come back on is jest a minor inconvenience as they is want to say.

As I git ready to turn into our driveway I notice a tree has come down in Stu Fench's back yard. Stu is out there with a chainsaw makin logs outta the thing. Stu lives two houses down from us on our side of the street. He's the manager of

Frankies in town. It's the old time grocery store where they rings up each item on the register. No fancy automatic zappin machines there. I park the Jimmy and walk over to see if I can be of any assistance.

"Hey, Stu, do ya need any help makin that there "far" wood?" I ask.

"Well, if you don't mind gittin some of these smaller branches outta my way I would be a might grateful" he says as he stops to wipe his brow. Stu ain't no youngin beings that he is only a couple a years away from retirement.

"Heck of a storm, eh?" I say as I grab a handful of small branches.

"Yep, and I hear Newie got it even worse," he replies.

"Jest came back from there and I'd say you got that right. We stopped at the ice cream shop and got pounded by the thing while we were there. It wuz me, Chester Dayrimple and Tom McFarlan trapped inside the place when the storm hit. Tom wuz goin to walk back to Possum when we ran into him at the shop. The hail wuz a half-inch deep. Covered ma Jimmy as well as other cars in the lot. Saw a bad wreck on the highway whilst we wuz comin home. Did you have any other problems here?"

"I did lose a few shingles and I'm worried about the rest of the roof. This has been a bad day all around. Let me git you a cold one and we can set a spell so I can tell you the bad news."

Stu hands me a cold beer and we pop the tops and take a slug. "Peters, who as you know is the owner of the Frankies, called me in today and said he'd be closin the store."

"Closin the store? What's the town goin to do for groceries?"

"Oh, that won't be no problem. See they are goin to build a new shoppin center on the Carson property jest outside town. Seems the Giant Falcon folks will be takin our place. It'll have a Mexican restaurant, shoe store, the Giant Falcon and a hardware place. Most likely a few others will want to locate there."

"Giant Falcon comin here?" I say as I take another drink of beer.

"Yeah, fraid so. Peters says there's no way he can compete with those fellas so he might as well close up. I'm pretty lucky though since I'm close to retarin anyhow. Man can't be a workin forever. Guess I'll be doin a lot more fishin now."

Giant Falcon is one of them super Super Markets. They done got everythin you could want in a store. You got a pharmacy, branch bank, dry cleaners, café and lots and lots of things to buy. We'll have to git used to them "mark of the beast" zappin registers. That's all they have in them big markets. Wonder what the preacher will do for groceries when the thing is the only store in town. Git used to it like everyone else I guess.

"Do you think the Norkle will be the bank there?" I question.

"No," Stu says as he finishes his beer, "they say it will be one of them big national banks. Some of them guys has got agreements to put a branch wherever Giant Falcon decides to build. It pays to be a big name operator in today's world."

"You can say her agin. Jest look at the folks who go to Newie for the Wal Marts. Made that trip myself jest to git a floor model oscillatin fan." I put down the can as I go back to helpin Stu with the tree. "I'm mighty sorry about Frankies closin and you losin that manager's job," I say as Stu starts up the chain saw again. He nods as he gits the thing a revin up full blast.

Stu and I make pretty quick work of that old tree. Bet he'll sure miss havin the shade of that there maple. Birds'll miss her too since that wuz a favorite nestin place for years. I finish rakin up more of the small stuff as Stu is stackin the logs he done cut.

"Mighty nice stack of wood ya got there."

"Yeah, that should make some nice warm fires in the fireplace but I think I would rather have the tree growin like she always did." Stu offers another cold one but I pass this time. "Looks like the power's come back on. I'd better git over and take that dern fan into the house for the wife. She's been a wantin that thing for a while now so she should be happy."

## Chapter X A Giant Comes to Town

I haul the box outta the Jimmy and take it into the house. Suzie Q (that's not her real name; it's Susan Marie, I jest been callin her Suzie Q since high school) greets me with a slight frown and says "where have you been? I saw the Jimmy's lights pull into the driveway an hour and a half ago."

"I jest been helpin old Stu with that tree that'd come down in his back yard."

"I've been worried near to death what with that bad storm and all."

That's jest like women fer ya, always worryin about somethin. They can't go with the flow like us menfolk. Lucky there's somebody to do the worryin in this world, jest glad I'm not the one.

Course I got to tell the story again about me and Chester and Tom and how we lucked out in the ice cream shop. I might a added a bit more dramatics about the fierceness of the storm and the dangers we had to endure. You gotta take every opportunity you git for havin the wife heap all sorts a sympathy on ya. That sorta takes the sting outta my delay in bringin the oscillatin floor fan inside. I unbox the thing and there's more gushin of gratitude. You got to know how to play the part of the big hero in situations like these. Now that the lights is back on I figger to play the hero onest agin by testin out the fan I done got for my sweetness. Now you can expect that an infernal gadget like this is not goin to come ready to use. "Some assembly is required." They always say that don't they? You got to lay out all the parts and check to see that

91

everythin is there and then git out your tools and set to work. Part A goes into Part B and you screws in Part C into Part D and make sure them screws is not too tight. You are missin Part E which is still in the box somewheres waitin to be found. After you go through all them details you finally got your fan. It makes you wonder why you is payin all this money when you have to do the work yourself. It says on the box, parts made in USA. If you can read the smaller print you find out it wuz partially assembled in China. OK, this means they made the parts; shipped them to China so some Chinese workers could "partially" put them together; then turned around and shipped the dern thing back to the USA for the consumer to "partially assemble" the final product. No wonder we got no work here. All they want Americans to do is "partially assemble" the thing they done paid for. The guy that thought up this nonsense is probably livin in a house on the beach sippin martinis all day. Why couldn't I have come up with this scheme?

The next day I decide to leave the pleasure of the air bein moved about by the oscillatin floor fan which yours truly has done masterfully "partially assembled." I want to go by the Carson property and see what's up. You can't sit idly by while the town is bein turned into a major shoppin extravaganza.

I cruise on out to the location and find things is already a buzzin. There is bulldozers and excavators and surveyors everywhere. Jumpin geewilikers they done already erected a big sign sayin future home of the Giant Falcon Plaza. They also has posted signs in several places sayin construction jobs available; see foreman in utility trailer.

Looks to me like these Giant Falcon folks is what you call cookin with gas. Either that or Mr. Peters at Frankies wuz aware of this deal afore he told everybody. Maybe he didn't want his managers decidin to move on afore the hurricane hit so to speak. That's a smart businessman keepin stuff to hisself, under his hat as some folks say.

Well, seein all those "help wanted" signs I decide to be a little nosey and see what this here's all about. I pass by a large sign indicatin the name of the project; S. T. Bikerton & Sons, general contractor, Newport, IL; the names of the architects; a list of sub-contractors and, of course, the typical EOE, EPA, FEMA, FDA, FBI and all those other gov ment agencies. You can't do nothin anymore without the Federal gov ment stickin its nose in to see if the air is fresh enough. No wonder they got so many workers in DC. They got to check on a buildin project in little ole Possum, WV the smallest town in the county of McCorkle. This here county ain't got but three towns and us and Pone together are not the size of New Hickory. Yes siree, gov ment offices and gov ment buildins and lawyers and judges and the like has taken over the entire country if you ask me and even if you don't.

Onest I reach the construction office trailer there's more signs tellin permit numbers and more help wanted; jobs available, see the project supervisor. They say "curosity killed the possum" but I'm willin to take the chance so I mosey on inside. "Howdy do?" I greet the foreman sittin behind a desk piled high with drawins and stuff. He sips from his coffee mug, looks up and says "Howdy. What can I do ya for?" You know he's the boss jest by noticin his clean shirt with his name over the pocket, that and the sign on the front of his desk sayin "R. J. Williams, project supervisor."

"Well," I say "Mr. Williams I couldn't help but notice all the "help wanted" signs you have here. Looks like a mighty big project."

"You lookin for work are ya?" he says as he's eyein me like a farmer checkin out a prize winnin bull at the county fair.

"Truth be told" I reply, "I wuz more than a might nosey bein a local resident here in Possum."

"Local, eh," he replies, "what gives around here? I've advertised all over the county and even checked with the unemployment office in New Hickory. Never seen workers so hard to find."

"Whatcha lookin for?" I say.

"Everything. We need laborers as well as skilled craftsmen. Pays good, up to $27.00/hour including benefits in some cases. Not many takers though."

"Mr Williams," I begin. He interrupts with "why not make it 'Bob' and you'd be?" as he offers his hand. Strong handshake. You can tell this guy is a genuine man. "Bob, then. I'm Clifford Paulsen, semi-retired I guess you'd say. Lived in Possum all my life. Been to Pittsburgh, Morgantown and onest to Charleston to see the boy's state championship basketball game. Possum won and I ain't had a reason to go back down there since. Know everybody in town, jest about." I pause to think over about what I'm goin to say next. "These folks around here are pretty settled in their ways. Onest you stops workin for your eats you can git dern comfortable in your situation, if you git my meanin."

"I think I might just be attuned to the channel you're broadcastin on," he says rather slowly and carefully. I guess that's midwestern talk for "I gits the message."

We chit chat a might longer about the project and the way things has been a changin since we wuz youngins. We say our goodbyes and I heads back out to the main highway. What a change this project is goin to make someday. I can't help but a thinkin how ole Possum has changed.

I don't reckon my grandfather would recognize this country if he were still livin. He came here knowin few folks and hopin to strike it rich. He and my grandma wuz willin to work hard at makin a new home in the USA. Grandpa Paulsen worked on construction sites and grandma took in washin and cleanin to make ends meet. They moved from place to place to find work and keep the eats comin to the youngins. Nine kids they had back in those times when you didn't always have a doctor and hospital close by home. Gittin sick back then wuz a major catastrophe. Two of those yougin died in their childhood. They were girls; the first and second born. Both were named Theresa. Back then they had no antibiotics and medical attention wuz quite primitive so to speak. Anyhow, the girls is buried up river near Pittsburgh. After the second girl died Grandma never went back to the name "Theresa." Someday I'm goin to search out that town and find the cemetery. I never knowed about them until a few years ago when I did some researchin on the family history. Grandma never spoke about them and my Grandpa died afore I wuz born. It wuz Aunt Virginia what done told me about them when she wuz up in years herself. The other seven had to live through the depression and World War Two. Most were born here in Possum after my Grandpa finally found this heavenly place to settle down.

Back then Possum wuz a boomin place. Folks wuz acomin here to take the jobs which were there for the askin. Grandpa decided this wuz the place where they found their heaven. Didn't know anyone here in Possum but he liked the town and quickly made friends. He finally decided to open a small grocery store and gas station. Seein's how these super Super Markets have gone into the gas sellin business today, Grandpa wuz way ahead of the times. There weren't many cars back then cause most folks rode the buses. What cars there wuz came to Grandpa's pumps and filled up their tanks. They stopped in at the store and bought their eats, mostly on credit then. Folks bought what they needed; spent some time shootin the breeze; partook of the free samples and came back on payday to put somethin down on their account. In the depression years Grandpa had to extend a lot of credit to townfolk. Big families were always hungry and money wuz always a problem. Possum survived though and Grandpa managed to have enough to raise his brood. He wuz astute when it comed to business deals and he managed to acquire property through the years. Built homes for the workers who always were lookin for a place to live close to work. You could walk to the mill and when the war came along there wuz plenty of jobs available agin. Them wuz the real boom times for Possum.

Things stayed that way until the late sixties. Workers at the mill were havin the greatest benefits a man could want. A lot of them done real well and it looked like it would never end. It did, though, when the foreign competition came along. It wuz slow at first but gradually grew and grew. Weren't long afore the layoffs started and work became scacrer than findin a real live possum in downtown Possum. The rest is history as folks like to say. Here we sit today wonderin if the good times will ever come back. Maybe this Giant Falcon project will be the real deal and we git back to livin the American dream instead of havin all this benefits stuff.

Drivin back I have to go by the old mill. There she sits idle. No cars in the parkin lot; no men hurrin to git inside to punch the clock; no smoke belchin from the furnaces. There's weeds poppin through the asphalt of the parkin lot which is criss-crossed with cracks because of the lack of maintenance. The windows has been broken out in many places and parts of the old roof are missin. What has our country come to that things like this exist? Onest this place put money into the hands of the workers and steel rolled out daily on semis. Now it sits, barren, broken and idle forever.

There's rumors that a big oil company is considerin locatin a facility here. It's one of them things that goes around town and nobody is quite sure where the info started. Makes sense though since there is activity on the Ohio side of the river what with the shale bein drilled. We got our share of the gas and oil down there deep inside the Marcellus. Quite a big bunch of drillers is workin the southern part of the state with much success. They has been buildin pipelines through the mountains to transport the gas to who knows where. Folks say if the drillin ever comes here we can git top dollar for leases on the land and royalties for the gas. Man, wouldn't that be a dream come true. Wished I had a hundred acres or so. I'd git rich like them guys down in Charleston. That's jest dreamin like you do when you're sittin on your porch and thinkin of fancy cars, big screen TVs, and the like. It's a way to pass the time when you git tired of lookin at the traffic go by.

## Chapter XI A Look at Possum

I find myself comin back into Possum proper if there is such a thing. We got old buildins where there used to be bustlin businesses. Right here on Washington Street, that's the main street in town, we have Mutzel's coffee shop. Old man Mutzel ran it for years and it wuz busy all the time. Folks stoppin in for coffee and pastries kept it goin day and night six days a week. Miss that ole place. Down the street is the old buildin where Nate Turner ran his bakery. You jest had to stop in every day for fresh baked bread and rolls. The smell of that bread bakin wuz a real enticement for a man jest come off his shift and on the way home. "Turn off you burners and buy it from Turners," folks used to say. It wuz catchy advertisin that even made visitors want to check in. Course ole man Jeff Cousins added a phrase of his own to help boost sales. "If you want to git busty, eat Turner's Crusty," he would say to the woman folk as he made his rounds deliverin bread to local grocery stores. We had five grocery stores back then. They all done disappeared along with Turner's Bakery as things got tight. Now jest Frankies is left and soon it will be gone.

There's the 5 & 10s; F W Woolworth, McCrorys, Mario's Pizza Pie Palace, Carpenter's Drug store, Rosenberg's department store, and Jackson's Chevrolet. Jackson's Chevy reminds me of Wilbur Motts who used to be a mechanic of sorts. One day on his day off he dressed in his Sunday's finest, had on a Fedora to add to the "upstanding citizen look"; jumped inside a car parked onside the highway jest as a bevy of workers wuz leavin the plant. Now in those days many folks used to walk back home or to the bus stop near the main gate. It wuz scortchin hot and if you rode the bus it would cost you ten cents and waitin in the hot sun for the bus wuz like addin heat to the fryin pan."Hey, fellas, would you like a ride back into town?" he asked. Ten cents wuz money in the bank so they readily agreed. "Hop in," he said, and they all piled inside.

Instead of startin the car, for which he had no key since it belonged to someone else, Wilbur commenced to turnin the steerin wheel from side to side as he imitated the sound of the car runnin. **"Vaarr, rrrrr, rrrr, ooom,"** he went as they grabbed the door handles and exited the car. Wilbur laughed for a long time over that one. Nobody ever owned up to bein one of the "riders." Wilbur wuz quite a character and really enjoyed playin practical jokes on jest about anybody in town. There wuz the time he "borrowed" a scarecrow fom a Halloween display. Wilbur crouched down behind some tall bushes alongside the highway comin into town. As a car came by, it jest happened to be the Mayor's, he tossed the dummy into the path of the auto. The brakes wuz a screechin and the Mayor quickly exited the car screamin "I didn't see the man. He ran out right in front of me. Is he dead? Call an ambulance! Call the sheriff!"

By then a small crowd had gathered and the antics of the frantic mayor runnin about and screamin caused a ripple of laughter to radiate through the onlookers. The mayor nearly had a heart attack when someone lifted an arm of the dummy and said "Yep, there ain't no life left here." Folks suspected Wilbur wuz the culprit but he had hightailed it out of the area afore the cops arrived. A search failed to find the guilty party and the mayor wuz transported to the hospital for observation. Years later Wilbur owned up to the deed inludin the "borrowin" of the scarecrow as a sort of deathbed confession.

Passin Carpenter's now, what a place that wuz for a kid. We used to go there and git lemon, cherry, and chocolate cokes. That wuz in the days when Coke wuz Coke and you didn't git all them flavors like today. Gittin a Coke meant gittin one of them funny shaped little glass bottles. They wuz ice cold when they wuz pulled from the cold water in the cooler. If the clerk didn't dry the bottle off you had to be real careful not to let it slip through your fingers. It wuz somethin you didn't git often and you knew it wuz goin to feel real good goin down on a hot summer's day. Carpenter's had the best chocolate malteds you ever did have. Man, they wuz so good you could taste them in your dreams. Plenty of malt and not skimpy on the ice cream. It wuz the real McCoy, not this fluffy, whipped stuff full of air and who knows what. They don't even have half-gallons of your favorite flavors anymore; they only sells those smaller tubs which is made to look like the real thing. No, today, you gits cheated when it comes to ice cream.

There's the old Ace Hobby Shop. Still has the signs in the windows for Lionel and American Flyer trains. Boy did a kid ever love that place. In the window they always had a giant P-40 Warhawk remote control airplane suspended from the ceiling. It was painted out in yellow camouflage which also had the big white stars in blue circles on the wing and fuselage indicatin it was pure USA. Razor sharp teeth on an open mouth were at the ready just below the engine and behind the tri-blade propeller.

Exhaust ports for the motor projected outward and toward the rear ahead of and just below the canopy.

Inside was seated a brave young pilot intently watching the controls. Those sharp teeth were the trademark of the famous Flying Tigers and we were certain they could destroy any enemy aircraft. What young lad couldn't see hisself in the pilot's seat ready to engage and shoot down any attacking Japanese Zeroes? Seein hisself a big ace hot on the tail of those Zeroes and bein a big hero? All the boys in the neighborhood could imagine the flames from the blasts of the machine guns and you could almost see the smoke from the fallin remains of your adversary's aircraft.

It looked like it wuz ready to fly right through the big front window of the Ace Hobby Shop. The wingspan musta been four feet, and with those large black rubber tires, could land smack dab safe in my back yard. We would stare at it and tell one another how we wuz goin to git enough money someday to buy that and take it down to the ball field and let her take-off for the clouds. None of us ever got enough money so it hung there until Mr. Franks decided to close the shop. Guess the plane got bought up in the auction since it disappeared when the store closed. We managed to git by with the balsa wood models which we all could afford. You jest slipped the wings through the fuselage and tossed them into the air. No fuel, no batteries, jest plain old air got them sailin. You had to be real careful the metal clip didn't fall off the nose. Losin that clip was like losin the engine off a real plane. End of your dreamin, it wuz.

Jack Trafford used to buy them plastic model plane kits and put them together. The Lockheed P38 Lightning, Grumman F6 Hellcat, Bell P39 Airacobra, North American F-86 Sabre Jet— he had 'em all. With the paint and decals they looked like the real thing. He had a hundred or so of them in his room. Well, maybe twenty-five to be honest. It looked like a lot to us kids. Jack went into the Air Force when he graduated. He wuz a pilot in the Vietnam War. After the war Jack didn't come back to Possum. His Ma still lives on Jefferson Street in the senior citizens apartments. She's up in years and her memory ain't what it used to be. Some people say Jack couldn't handle it when he knowed his Ma wuz that way. There wuz others what claimed he worked for the CIA when he left the Air Force and wuz overseas on a secret mission.

Duffy's bar is still here; one of the oldest in town. The bar sits between Kincher's Hardware store and the old Grimm's Grocery store. Both are closed now. Don't know if it wuz lack of parkin or lack of customers which pulled the plug on them. Good old Duffy's wuz really popular in spite of it all back when. Duffy used to run a small local brewery at the other end of town. Duffy's Pale Ale wuz the name of the brew and it wuz a favorite around town. If you go there now you'll see the remains of the old stone buildin where the bottlin went on. Time wuz when the kegs and bottles couldn't git outta there fast enough. Townsfolk said it wuz the best beer available. Course they wuz kinda partial to it since it wuz brewed in Possum. You can stop in the bar today and always find some locals drinkin away their checks. It's quite busy when they gits their benefits. Sheriff always gits a lottta them "domestic abuse" calls about the same time of month.

The Pink Garter is another drinkin place in town which is popular with the locals. You'll find the regular characters there listenin to tales of woe and cryin in their beer. If they spent as much time doin somethin useful as they did drinkin maybe they'd have less to cry about. As you can probably tell, I don't particularly care for that place. Stokes, the owner, has always served up a mess a peanuts. You know the kind I mean, salted in the shell. The more folks eat the more beer they want. Those shells git tossed all over the floor of the place. If you're foolish enough to go into that place you got to step on them shells wherever you go. They do serve up a good burger and some other sandwiches but who wants to wade through a zillion peanut shells? What does he think I am, an African elephant for Pete's sake. I guess there is some attraction since they have some mighty fine lookin waitresses workin there.

I knowed a fella, Mike Vulcasic, who wuz a pretty regular customer at one time. He had a hankerin for a waitress named Genevieve. Mike wuz not much of a drinker and never cared for the peanuts cause he didn't have no teeth. Not jest false teeth; not a few teeth missin but absolutely none. Mike would have to gum his food if it weren't liquid. His usual order wuz graham crackers and milk. Stokes kept a supply of them since Mike stopped in every day after work. Course it wuz understood that Genevieve would always be his waitress. If she had a day off, he would jest pop in and say he wuz passin through. Onest he decided to take her out for lunch and of course, they went to the Pink Garter. Genny had a burger and beer and Mike had the usual. That there wouldn't be too excitin ceptin when they sat at the table Mike said they wuz settin "knees to knees." That definitely wuz as much excitement as Mike had ever had. He told the story to jest about anyone who wuz listenin. After that, Mike always called Genny his "girl." She never did comment on the excitement of the date but always remained his waitress until he croaked from a heart attack. Guess it must have been more than a lonely heart could withstand havin that romance of "knees to knees."

There's the old Rosenberg's department store. Nothin but butcher paper coverin the windows now. Used to be the number one store in town. "Three rooms for $398.00" wuz their slogan and they furnished about every place in town. The ladies would git all dressed up on Saturdays and spend quite a few bucks of the hubbie's paycheck there. As a kid I went there with my mom and waited as she rifled through the rack of dresses and coats lookin for a bargain. It wuz fun for me cause I knowed she would take me to Carpenter's for a Coke or malted after the shoppin wuz done. Them neighbor ladies wuz always stoppin to pat me on the head and tell mom how I wuz agrowin like a ragweed. It weren't bad, though, since they looked real pretty all dressed up with their bonnets. They smelled good, too, since old man Rosenberg gave them a good sprayin with the latest fragrance of them perfumes he wuz a sellin. He wuz quite the promoter. Ladies always ended up with bags of goodies to take home onest they left the store. He had a kid's department on the second floor where everyone bought school clothes and stuff for dressin up on Sunday. Back then you had to look your best when you went to Sunday services at church. There wuz none of this wearin blue jeans and shorts when you attended. You didn't do no fussin or spunkin onest you got to church. Mom or Dad would give you that look which meant a sound spankin if you didn't straighten up and behave like they told you. Kids today crawls around bangin their toys and eatin their cereal or cookies while the preachin is goin on. That is the ones that goes to church at all.

Speakin of churches you won't find as many today in Possum as we had in days gone by. Lots of nationalities had their own churches back then. There wuz the Serbian, the Greek, the French Catholics, the Eyetalian Catholics, the Polish Catholics, and the Slovakian Catholics in addition to the Lutheran, the Presbyterian, the Methodist, and the Gospel Hall.

The Hall was always the loudest place on Sundays. People shoutin and singin and "praisin the Lord". Little Jimmy Wernok claimed they got down on the floor and rolled up the aisle in a trance of sorts, speakin in strange tongues. Onest us kids went over and listened outside the open windows. We heard strange noises to be sure but I can't say which tongue they were a speakin in. Only Pastor Roth could be heard to actually "speak" any words and they be in plain English. Somethin about "lipstick and rouge was goin to send you straight to the clutches of Satan in Hell."

I may have missed some but you can see we had our share of churches. People used to say "Possum, the town of churches and bars." Between the two they out numbered any businesses in our town. Sometimes a preacher would come to town and set up a tent on the ball field to conduct a revival service. There wuz a lot a preachin and singin and folks gittin saved durin the things. Course after the things wuz over and the men got back to work there wuz a backslidin. Menfolk had a tough life and it wuz easy for old habits to worm their way back into their hearts. But folks had somethin they believed in and wuz uplifted even if but for a short while. Now these kids today is scarcer than possums in Possum in any of the churches what is left. Seems a shame that them old ways is gone.

## Chapter XII News Aplenty

I decide to take a break and git a cold one afore I git back home. My Jimmy slides into the parkin lot of Schufty's where there seems to be a good crowd on hand by the looks of the cars in the lot. It's an old favorite beins it has been operatin for quite a few years. You need a minute to adjust to the lightin inside as Schufty has always kept it cozy dark. Darkness helps to highlight the neon bar signs he has all above the bar. You name it and you'll find it at Schufty's. "Bud," "Miller," "Coors Lite," "Old Frothingslosh," "Heinekin," "Blue Moon," "Moosehead" are but a few of the multi-colors which grace the room. Good eats too. Matter of fact, he has a large flashin sign out front of the place which says only one thing "EAT." That may be a sign advertisin the food he serves or it may jest be a command tellin you what to do when you gits inside. There's all kinds of taxidermy on the walls since Walt Shufty is an avid hunter and fisherman. He's always made trips to Canada so you'll find a moose head, northern pike, bass, a lake trout as well as white tail deer heads mounted on all sides. He's mighty proud of the sixteen point buck he got down state one year. You don't want to git him started tellin you about all them huntin and fishin trips he's taken. Shufty talks a mile a minute and seldom lets up for a breather. He'll tell you the exact location, the weather condition, which way the wind wuz a blowin for any one of them you inquire about. Locals know better than to bring up that topic.

Well, I finds a quiet table and settle down for a brew. Katie comes by and takes my order. "How about somethin to eat with that?" she asks.

Now that she mentions it I am a bit hungry.

"Give me the Shufty burger with fries and slaw," I reply. She jots it down and heads for the back.

Bout that time Slim Wilson comes by my table and says "Well, Cliff Paulsen, fancy meetin you here." Oh, no, I think, Slim is lookin for a free beer. "You been out shoppin or doin chores for the old lady?" he asks.

"Neither. Took a ride to take a look-see at the construction on the Carson property."

"Now ain't that somethin else?" he offers as he pulls out a chair. "Mind if I set a spell?" Afore I can answer he is seated across from me. We went to school together and we both worked at the brick yard after graduation. He is more of what you would say is an acquaintance than an old school chum but I don't mind the company since he keeps an ear tuned to what's goin on in town.

"I been down there myself checkin things out. Put in an application for some construction work. Boss man says they needs a bunch a workers for that project."

"You goin to go to work on the Giant Falcon Plaza are ya?" I query.

"Nah, I jest want to see what they say when they look at my application. Pay is not bad but I can't afford to give up my current situation if you gits my meanin. Sides they say we is goin to git a new gas plant very dern soon."

Now that is some news. I question Slim to see if he really has the inside scoop on rumors that has been goin round.

"What have you heard? Is the shale processin plant comin to Possum for sure?" I ask rather excitedly.

"Well, don't quote me on this or nuthin, but the word is we is definitely in line to git the dern thing. They are buyin everythin south of the new Plaza for potential construction beginnin as early as this spring."

"Ah, there's been rumors for months about that stuff. Don't put a lotta faith in it myself," I say. My bluff has worked. Slim is eager to tell me more. I jest needs to do a little listenin now.

"Don't repeat a thing I'm goin ta tell ya. You can keep a little secret under your hat can't ya?" Slim says as he lowers his voice. I have to move my chair in a bit closer to hear over the music that's blarin about lonely hearts and lost love. "I got a scoop that nobody else in town has yet heard."

I nod in agreement as he asks "can ya keep this quiet till the news comes out? Ya gotta swear on your pap's grave." I nod again. "I wuz a drinkin with Danny Weissmuller the other day when he had a few too many and he let it slip that he done bought up all that farm property south of the new plaza. Sez he has got a deal to sell it at a premium price to the Marcellus shale people. They intend to build their cracker plant right there. It's all set. Big important people has put their John Henry's on the dotted line. Commissioner Weissmuller is goin to make a handsome profit and all he had to do wuz a bit of paperwork."

"Wow, that is big news. Wouldn't you know that Danny would find a way to profit from the whole thing."

Slim gits quiet as Katie brings my order. "Slim, how about a cold one on me?" I ask. A beer is a small price to pay for this info.

"Okay, but jest one. Make it a Coors Lite."

"Anythin to eat?" Katie inquires. Oh, no, I can jest imagine Slim decidin on a thick steak well done, with a loaded baked tater and with onion rings to boot. Slim glances at me as if to see if it's OK and I nod approval. I've gone this far so I might as well roll the dice, 'sides I would like a little more info.

"Chili, a bowl of your chili with onions and cheddar. Hot sauce on the side."

Whoa, have I hit the lotto or what? "Chili and a beer?" This inside info for chili and a beer! It's gotta be my lucky day.

When Katie leaves, Slim starts talkin again. Now Slim really shoulda been a news reporter; he loves nothin more than to git in on all that's news in town. He gits that look that says "I got some news that you would love to hear. Not only that but nobody else in town has even a hint of what I know." He gits a great deal of pleasure of watchin the expression on your face when he drops the bomb on you; sometimes, like this, it is an atomic bomb.

"This here news is good as gospel. Danny has deeds to all those lots in his pocket. I got the impression that Judge DiPetro is the money man behind his deal. You know Danny and the judge are tighter than a snake wrapped around a blueberry bush waitin for a nice fat blue jay to come along."

"So that's why the Giant Falcon people are buildin that plaza?" I inquire.

"Dern tootin. They know onest the oil plant is built the town will git back to boomin." He says with a broad smile on his face. You know the symmetrical kind like they uses in advertisin. Slim don't qualify for that stuff since he got those missin teeth smack dab in the front of his mouth.

We git on with the eatin and chattin and the news gits a little less excitin. Slim knows who's been cheatin on their wives; how well various businesses in town are doin and who will be named the new coach of the Pone football team. Seems the likely candidate is a cousin of one of the county commissioners. Slim says he knows some about the game but his main credential is bein a relative of commissioner Schwartzfeld. Now that don't beat all! It sure pays to git into politics in this state. Most folks run the other way when you bring up any kind of political talk but the smart ones knows it is the path to riches. Folks here hold to the old ways and stick to the tag of the politics their pappy done told them. You know, the rich Republicans is never for the people and the Democrats is always lookin out for the little fella. They is lookin out all right but their main interest is their own pocketbooks.

Commissioners know they is pretty well set onest they is in office since folks jest go on votin the straight party ticket. I always thought it wuz a big mistake that votin wuz not restricted. How can you expect folks who is gittin a check for doin nuthin to vote against themselves? Take Lori Sue. She's gottin herself a septic system, a new well and brand spankin new roof on her place. Her check runs $700.00 a month and her medical needs is all met, includin transportation. Her only concern is that dern Lulu. No wonder she showers that dog with fillet mignons and baked taters. I don't remember the last time I ate one of those myself. Do you expect that Lori Sue will vote to give all that up? Yet her vote done counts as much as yours and mine. The best you can do is cancel hers. Fact is though, there's gittin to be many more like her than those doin honest work. Guess who wins!

We been here for quite a while so I figger it's time to hit the road for home. "Well, Slim," I say as I count out my money for the check, "bout time I git back home to Suzie Q. Been a pleasure meetin up with ya AND my lips are sealed. You can count on it."

"Oh, I knowed I can trust ya, 'Champ' you've always been the quiet type. Heck, I never knowed you to go blabbin anythin when we wuz in school."

I wuz the quiet type in school all right. My Mama done told me when I entered First Grade, "Keep quiet, sit still and don't make no trouble." She only had to tell me onest and I knew what I should do. I surely knew that big black "licorice stick" was left hangin there on the back of the pantry door after Dad took off his belt.

Slim calls me 'Champ' ever since I won medals in the county track meet my senior year. Records still stand to this day. Not many folks remember back then other than Slim, least no one else calls me 'Champ'.

## Chapter XIII Possum Rebirth

As I go to git back in the Jimmy, I spot Wally Mugford approachin, wavin his arms. He's holdin that dern "cell phone" to his ear so I can't imagine what he's up to now. "Hold up a cotton pickin second" he hollers as he approaches. He takes the cell phone down and stuffs it in his pocket.

"Wally, why are you playin around with that worthless cell phone?" I holler at him.

"Oh, this ain't no fake cell phone. This is one of them Obama phones. Got it for free at the tent store in front of Frankies. They is givin them out for free to lots of folks as long as you is on the disability or welfare. You git 1500 minutes of talk time and 1500 of textin every month. Obama is payin for all this so it don't cost us nuthin."

"Wally, Obama ain't payin for nuthin. Us Possums are payin for them dern things, at least the folks what are workin for a livin. You had jest as well go to your neighbor's house and stick a gun to his head and say 'I wanna cell phone and you is gotta pay for it.'" I say rather angrily.

"Gee, that don't sound like a good idea after all. Bet them other folks at Frankies never thought of that neither. Them folks at the tent make it sound so good, it's all free and that," he says in a sorrowful voice. "Wow, you almost made me forget, I got a message for ya from Suzie."

"Suzie Q called you on that thing did she?" I say rather sarcastically.

"Oh, no, I seen her over at the house a couple hours ago and she asked if I had seen ya in town. She offered me five bucks if I look around town for ya. Havin nothin of particular importance to do at that moment and needin a buck or two, I took her up on the deal. If I seen ya, I wuz sposed to tell ya that the post office tried to deliver a package for her but it had some restriction on it. Anyhow they have it down at the post office and she would like you to stop in and git it. She had to go over to Francine's so's she couldn't git it herself. I'm glad I found ya cuz I would hate to give this money back. You is a hard guy to find so I guess I earned my money."

"Don't worry, Wally, you can keep the five bucks. I'm glad you found me here. I'll jest walk over to the post office and check it out."

Wally asks if I'd mind if he walked along since he had nothin particular to do at the moment. I can't see the harm in it so I say "jest as long as you don't be holdin that dern cell phone. I can't stand for folks to be talkin while they is walkin." He readily agrees and keeps pace as we enter the post office door. I see postmaster Collins at the service window and step up since there is no line waitin.

"Got a package for us do you, Tim," I inquire.

"Sure enough, Cliff," he says as he heaves a large box out the door marked "employees only." I can immediately see that the package has been damaged in the mail. One end looks like an elephant happened to git loose in the back of the mail truck and took out his anger on my box.

"The dern thing came this way and we thought you'd better check it out afore we left it," Tim says as he lays it on the floor.

Wally suddenly pipes up "do you suppose it's somethin valuable?"

"Nah," I say, "this here's somethin Susie Q ordered from the shoppin channel I'll bet." I reach in to the smashed end and pull out part of a faux marble bust. The head has been cracked in two right down the middle.

"What **THAT** is?" Wally asks me real nosey-like? "It's what's left of a bust of Mozart," I say.

"Mozart, which president wuz he?" Wally questions.

"He weren't no president, he wuz a music composer," Tim chimes in.

I dig out the rest of the broken pieces and find the other bust of Beethoven which is undamaged. "I think she ordered these things for the mantle. Guess she is goin to have to return this and wait for a while."

Tim says he can mark it as 'damaged upon receipt' and return to sender.

"Yeah" Wally speaks up, "you don't have to take that. This is not Russia. This here is the United States of America."

"That'll be okay, Tim, I'll let the wife know what happened. She may even decide to cancel the sale and save me some bucks." Still my lucky day I think to myself as we exit the post office.

I climb into the Jimmy and wave so long to Wally, who by now has pulled out his Obama phone and begins speakin to who knows. I ain't in no hurry to git back home now that I don't have the gall dern package. Anyway, Suszie Q is probably still over at Francine's place jibber-jabberin about somethin.

Francine is her older sister who lives a few streets down from us. She's what you call a widow since she done lost her husband, Dr. Frank Thompson. It wuz quite a shock to everyone in town when we heard the news. Dr. Frank wuz a fine man, well liked, and kind to townsfolk. Plenty of people didn't have the cash on hand when they wuz in need of medical services. Dr. Frank always said "don't you be a worryin about it none, you can pay me when you git your funds." A good many people never 'got the funds.' It didn't make no nevermind to Dr. Frank. He always welcomed them when they came back in again. He wuz ony fifty-nine years of age and seemed quite healthy to look at him. Told Francine he wuz goin to take a break for a few minutes and went in to lie down. When he didn't git up for supper she went into the livin room to call him. That's when she found him on the sofa lookin like he wuz fast asleep. Trouble wuz she couldn't wake him cause he had done died right there. She wuz a bit hysterical when she called me and Suzie Q to come over quick. We rushed over but it wuz obvious he wuz already gone. The coroner said it wuz natural causes, probably a heart attack.

Didn't seem possible that a man that healthy would go like that. He wuz always joggin or ridin his bicycle through town. He was a real health freak. Always exercisin and watchin his eats. Never around second hand smoke if he could help it. 'Twern't but a week after he ran in the county marathon. Wuz a top ten finisher to boot. Yep, Dr. Frank will be missed in Possum.

We have only one doctor left in Possum now, Dr. John Vickers. There are three dentists left so there must be quite a need for tooth extractin and fillins and dentures. They all seem to be doin well for themselves. All of them have offices downtown and they live pretty close to our neighborhood. I always kid our dentist, Dr. Tom Lancere, about how I'm goin to strike it rich someday. Next tooth I lose will go under my pillow and the tooth fairy will leave me the winnin ticket on the lotto. When I git my millions, I'll buy that big house next door to him and see if I can't smoke him out with my barbecue. Trouble is, Dr. Tom don't let me lose any teeth lately so I have nothin to leave under the pillow. Do you suppose Dr. Tom jest doesn't want me for a neighbor?

I take the long way around to go to Francine's house. No need to rush since I know the two of them will probably be still talkin. I pass by the small park the town holds in high regard. The Fourth of July parade always ends up at that spot and the school bands play a medley of patriotic songs. School kids go to the park to play and have fun. The park has a tall flag pole with Old Glory proudly wavin in the strong breeze. There's also smaller poles for the West Virginia state flag and the Possum city flag which wuz designed by school kids back in the 1970s. It's a white flag with a purple border and a purple possum in the center.

This small park sets overlookin the big bend in the mighty Ohio River. People refer to it as Union Park since it wuz established around the Abraham Lincoln tree so many years ago. The Lincoln tree sets in the very center of the park and accordin to legend wuz planted there on the day Mr. Lincoln passed by on the railroad across the river in Ohio. That little oak tree has growed into a magnificent tree today. If that tree could talk it would have quite a story to tell of the events it has seen. Why, there wuz World Wars, boom times, the great depression, radio, TV, men takin off in flyin machines and eventually flyin right up to the moon itself. Yep, that tree has seen 'em all and has jest kept addin rings that contain the story of its growth.

There are flower beds spread all around which are planted every spring and tended by townsfolk. Somethins bloomin there through all seasons of the year. My favorite is the red and white carnations but them purple irises is a real eye catcher. It is usually a very quiet place except when the Fourth of July parade is organized around it. Union Park is much smaller in size than Possum Park that the Warner family begun. Union never wuz intended to have critters housed there. Ain't big enough for no ball fields or large picnic tables. It just exists as a reminder of bygone days when we first became our own state.

That name, Abraham Lincoln tree, is what folks call the tree. City finally placed a plaque in front of it statin it for a fact in 1960. Don't recall when the name first got started. Perhaps when Mr. Lincoln wuz murdered by that rat of a man, John Wilkes Booth. It don't seem right that a skunk of a man could shoot a US President in the back of the head whilst he sat enjoyin a play with his wife. Sure caused a lot of problems with that bullet.

Various claims are made as to who actually planted the tree. Guess we'll never know. The city later installed busts of Lincoln, Grant, Sherman and Sheridan in 1909 as part of the celebration of Lincoln's birthday. They stand today as a reminder of our state's creation by our famous president. He wuz cheered by townsfolk after his election especially because there weren't never no slaves in Possum. Folks like to sit on the concrete benches and take in the beauty of the park. It's a nice place to spend a few quiet moments. The amazin thing is that the park has never had litter to speak of. Everyone in town appreciates the beauty of the park and litterin the place would be unthinkable. The park is probably on a par with the football team when it comes to bein a town favorite.

I turn the corner where I catch sight of the Thompson home. The place sits a ways back from the street and has lovely gardens and shrubbery. I see Francine's silver BMW in the driveway and pull in right behind. "Anybody home" I say as I ring the large brass bell hangin by the front door. The sound attracts the attention of the two inside who come immediately to the door. We exchange our "howdy doos" and enter the livin quarters. It is finely furnished as you would expect for a doc's house. Francine pours a glass of iced tea for me and we proceed to the patio area.

"Did you pick up the package at the post office?" Suzie Q inquires.

"Nope. The gall dern thing wuz smashed in transit."

"Oh, no," Suzie says as she almost begins to tear up.

"Mozart wuz smashed beyond repair. Beethoven arrived in good shape but what good is one of them things when you needed two? I told Tim to return it to the shoppin channel."

"Why didn't you bring home the Beethoven?" she asks.

"Like I said, the box wuz badly damaged and I figgered that what good is one when you wanted two. You can always reorder if you don't want a refund."

"I'll have to reorder them next time they are on sale, that is if they don't send a replacement."

"Willikers." I think to myself. I thought we were blessed that the package wuz crushed and now she is goin to reorder them dern things. Well, at least they will be on the mantle and not where I will have to spend time lookin at em.

As I take a big drink of the tea Suzie Q changes the subject. "What would you think about livin in Alaska?"

"Alaska" I repeat. "Why don't you ask about the south pole or next door to the Man in the Moon or the planet Mars even? Why the heck would we want to go to Alaska?"

"Now afore you git on your high horse and dismiss the idea I think you should listen to what Francine has to say."

Okay, now I got to listen to her sister try to convince me to go somewhere I don't wanna go jest so I can be called "polite." I know I'll never hear the end of it unless I relent so I sit back and say, "All right, give it a shot. My ears are wide open."

Francine is sittin in her best pose. Looks like one of them TV news reporters they hire to attract the male audience. She folds her hands in her lap and gits that simple symmetrical smile on her face when she is about to give it to ya but good.

"Well," she begins, "you recall that Frank and I took a tour of Alaska four years ago. Frank said it was one of the most thrilling adventures he's ever had. I mean the views were just spectacular. The mountains reaching down to the sea in

Anchorage, the amazing ocean wildlife, the national park and the food was just out of this world. We took an unbelievable train ride from Anchorage to Fairbanks with a stop over in Denali National Park. That train ride alone was enough to make you fall in love with the place."

It's gittin real thick now and I can tell that it is goin to git much thicker afore we are through. I've knowed Francine since high school and she always had that gift of gab.

"Frank probably told you about the absolutely fabulous fishing trip we made shortly after we arrived in Anchorage. We flew in this little teeny tiny plane where Frank had to sit beside the pilot since the plane held so few people. The views were marvelous although the ride was just a bit bumpy. When the plane started to descend after a couple of hours flying time, I looked out of the window and said 'my goodness gravy, there's no airport in sight.' Well, they do things differently in Alaska. The plane went down and landed right on the river. Took us straight to the lodge where we found our accommodations ready for us. Frank went out on the river for salmon fishing but I stayed back to enjoy the natural beauty of the place. He actually caught a large salmon and had it flown back to the lower forty-eight."

"I do recall that, Francine," I interject, "we came over and ate some of that delicious fish."

"Well, but of course you did. I do remember preparing that fish and how much you and Suzie enjoyed it. What wonderful memories that brings to my mind."

Suzie Q is sayin nuthin; jest sittin there smilin and noddin her head on occasion.

"So I know you had a wonderful time but what has that got to do with movin to Alaska?" I question Francine.

"Absolutely everything," she says as her simple smile broadens. "I've got to thinking how the three of us should take one of those tours just as Frank and I did. Just the three of us, so we could do some scouting on a good place to live. I just don't think I want to spend the rest of my life in this old town of Possum with its one foot in the grave and about to die. There is nothing left here for us anymore."

"Jest the three of us?" I say as my voice goes up a notch. "Them cruise ships hold five thousand people or so. I couldn't be cooped up with a bunch of them big city types. They knows everythin; they is livin in the best places on earth; they can't believe a person could live a day in a place like Possum. Them folks regard us as fly-over territory; we exist and that's all they know about us. Can't imagine why anyone would want to spend a day jostled around by them snooty city types who's probably got bed bugs or TB or cookamonga disease or some other unwanted critters."

"Now sweetness, it can't be all that bad," the wife finally peeps up. "Sweetness!" She only calls me that when she is a wantin somethin pretty bad. This is not lookin good. It is two against one and I'm already "sweetness."

Francine commences with her persuasive spiel—at least for Suzie Q—what's she goin to call me next after takin in all this stuff?

"Possum is just a place of sad memories to me now. The town is going absolutely nowhere. I just can't stand the thought of spending my last days here without Frank. He loved Alaska. Said maybe we could go there to live after he retired. It would be such a wonderful opportunity for the three of us."

"Francine," I butt in, "it may be a wonderful opportunity for you and I know jest how you are feelin. Time heals all wounds and besides I don't think Possum is all that bad."

"Not all that bad," she blurts out as she looks like she's about to cry. "This town is dried up and done for. Just look around yourself. There's nothing left here but ramshackle buildings and a population without anything to look forward to. Most are satisfied with the lifestyle they have and they have no desire to change things for the better. They have already given up."

I stop her afore she is about to start another sentence. "Francine, you've got to give it time. Like I said, the town is not dead yet. Maybe a sickly patient but nothin some fresh blood injection won't cure." I'm thinkin about the news Slim gave me a short while ago but know better than to open my mouth to Francine. The news would race about town like a wild fire knowin Francine as I do. "Tell you what, Suzie Q and I need to do some thinkin and talkin afore we make any big moves to Alaska. I promise you we will have a serious investigatin of this here matter. We may even need to sit down with you and go over a few things onest more. Meantime you jest sit tight and don't do no frettin over this. Why don't you come over to our place tomorrow for dinner and bring your album of Alaska pictures. I jest ain't in no rush to give up on Possum jest yet."

"Perhaps you're right. We don't need to rush into this. I am sorry but it seemed like such a good idea to me when Suzie and I were talking. You've got a deal. I'll be over tomorrow and I'll bring the photos Frank took. After you look at them you may change your mind."

"Excellent," I say as I finish the iced tea. "Suzie Q and I have got to head on out for now but we'll be lookin forward to seein you tomorrow." There's hugs all around and Suzie Q and "sweetness" walk out to the driveway. "My dear," I say as I open her door and motion with a sweep of my hand for her to enter. "See ya tomorrow," we say to Francine as we back down the drive and wave good bye.

Suzie Q begins cryin as soon as we git jest a few houses away. "Poor Francine, she is totally lost without Frank. She wuz dependin on him for everythin. Now she has to close up things at the office and take care of all his affairs. She misses him so very much. Those two were like sugar and cream. I never dreamed that they would be separated like this. I expected they would grow old together and live out their retirement. I can see them livin in Alaska now."

"Life doesn't always go accordin to the book, Suzie Q," I interrupt. "We all expect that little baby we is holdin will grow up to be an adult someday and live out his life till he grows too old for livin. You know it don't always come true. Remember the Mackey family. They done lost two boys in the war and another to drivin drunk. Dead afore they's twenty-five years of age and without no proper time for grievin in between. Sure they thought them boys would be there to help 'em in their elder years. Life don't have to obey no fairness rules like the gov ment tries to make. Life jest is, jest like road kill happens."

As we drive futher, Suzie Q decides to make one last pitch. "You know, sweetness, Francine's idea of Alaska as a place to call home is worth givin some thought. Possum is dead after all and a body's got to think what they can do for their twilight years."

There's that "sweetness" comin back into the conversation so I knows to be extry careful.

"I jest can't see myself leavin Possum," I say. "I done lived here all my life. Don't never saw no place I ever cared more for. I expect someday to die here even if I never seen that Grand Canyon or El Paso or any of them other excitin places. This is my home. There is no other place like it on earth. Livin here is all a man can dream about. The world out beyond has got Hollywood, New York and Chicago with all them fancy people with their fancy electronic gizmos. They is too busy commutin to work, payin high prices for everythin and barely have the time for livin like a body was meant to. God made Possum. Man created the outside world.

Grandpappy tried all them places out and put his foot down right here in McCorkle county. As for bein dead that is a matter of speculation. I speculate that Possum is not dead. It might a had a sickness that did it a lotta harm but I see it comin back to life. We is goin to have a town we can be proud of onest again."

"Do you really believe that, Possum will come back?" Suzie questions me.

"I said it, didn't I? Why do you think the Giant Falcon Plaza is bein built? Do you think them smart big city folks with the high IQs and degrees from Harvard goes around buildin plazas cause they feels an urge to do some buildin somewheres? No, they has done a survey of the area. They knows what the future of the place looks like. They is out to make money, big money. Big things are comin to Possum, jest you wait and see."

"I hope you're right. I want to believe, I really do," Suzie Q says.

Almost afore she can git her words out I brake hard for a critter crossin the street. "Did you see that?" I question her.

"What wuz that thing? I jest caught it outta the corner of my eye," she shrieks in a loud, excited voice.

"That THING," I reply, "wuz nothin less than a real live possum!"

"A **POSSUM**?" she cries out.

"Yep, and that'd be the sign. Jest like when old Noah McCorkle founded this town. The critter crossed our path jest like back then. Heaven has done told us that this is where heaven is. This is where we is meant to be"

## The E..

**Oops**, not so fast my dear reader. That little critter crossing the road is not *"The End"* but the start of a new cycle of life. Things have been running in cycles since the beginning of time. Perhaps that Big Bang was nothing more than a cycle which had to cease so a new cycle could begin. Let us hope that like it the cycles for Possum and for America continue well into the future with many blessings for our children and grand children.

## Epilogue

You've read my story and I hope you have come to love the town as I do. There is, however, one last thing I got to tell.

Don't you be lookin up Possum Crossing, WV in no gall dern Atlas or on that Google Maps. Same goes for McCorkle County and Pone and New Hickory. You won't find them no matter how hard you look. Go ahead, git one of them big city private investigators if you want. Nobody is goin to find us.

West Virginia is said to be "Almost Heaven." Well, Possum is Heaven. It is a place of the heart and the mind. Oh, the stories that be told is all true incidents what happened in real life here in America. Possum exists everywhere in the USA cause this story is the story of what has happened to this once great country.

Don't git me wrong. It is still the best place on earth and there is no place I'd rather be but we've been driftin from our intended course. The proud, independent, hard working people have been let down by the gov ment what leads them. It's our fault, of course, since we let it happen. We got comfortable and distracted by technical gadgets which took our eyes off the true purpose of our country. Can we get it back? Will we git it back? The answer depends on <u>We the People.</u> Like Possum there is a chance to return to glory. We must demand it or see further decay and loss of freedom.

In a modern day scene The Ohio River flows lazily between Ohio and West Virginia. No longer does the mighty river choose its own path as it rushes westward to the Mississippi. Giant dams constructed to control the waters and aid commercial traffic hold back the flow and direct its course.

The river seen in the center of this photo looks almost lake-like placid. Let there be downpours and she will no longer retain this appearance. In a bid to show her mighty power she will once again overflow her banks and take back what is hers even if but for a short while.

As has been the case for centuries her waters mark the beginning of America's first westward territories. The Ohio dutifully stands sentinel as the guardian of the natural boundary between states. Upon her back flowed men and supplies taking aim at the Mississippi and the Wild West.

Printed in the United States
By Bookmasters